A Forgiving Kind

A Forgiving Kind

By

Angela K Parker

A Forgiving Kind
Copyright © 2019 by Angela K. Parker
All Rights Reserved.

Without limiting the rights under copyright reserved above, no part of this publication may be reproduced, stored in, or introduced into a retrieval system, or transmitted, in any form, or by any means electronic, mechanical, photocopying, recording, or otherwise, without the prior written permission of the author of this book.

This is a work of fiction. Names, characters, businesses, places, events, and incidents are either the products of the author's imagination or used in a fictitious manner. Any resemblance to actual persons, living or dead, or actual events is purely coincidental.

Published: Angela K. Parker 2019
angelaparkerauthor@gmail.com

"Cover Design © Dark Water Covers"
ISBN: 978-1095708590

Dedication

To the heartbreakers of the world that aren't afraid to change, and the strong-minded individuals with the will to forgive them.

Table of Contents

Chapter 1	1
Chapter 2	9
Chapter 3	15
Chapter 4	22
Chapter 5	30
Chapter 6	41
Chapter 7	48
Chapter 8	57
Chapter 9	67
Chapter 10	75
Chapter 11	83
Chapter 12	89
Chapter 13	97
Chapter 14	107
Chapter 15	117
Chapter 16	122
Chapter 17	129
Chapter 18	136
Chapter 19	143
Chapter 20	149

Chapter 21	156
Chapter 22	163
Chapter 23	170
Chapter 24	175
Chapter 25	181
Acknowledgments	187
Author's Note	188
Until Next Time...	188
About the Author	189
Connect with the Author	190

Chapter 1

Bradley

It's been two weeks since I convinced Val to come along with me on this business trip. I didn't know it at the time, but she really was the best choice. Her work is remarkable. The time we've spent together has been mostly professional. Aside from an occasional lunch, Val seems reluctant to be around me out of respect for Sam, I suppose.

Sam.

I still feel horrible about the way I left. The look on her face when I told her that I had to go away for one month threatened to melt me from the inside out. I couldn't tell her the whole story. So, I omitted an important truth. It seemed like the best decision at the time, but now I'm not so sure.

I was torn.

I couldn't leave her with the thought that Val, my ex-girlfriend, would be alone with me for the next month. It's a thought that I wouldn't be okay with if the roles were reversed.

And I couldn't leave Val behind to become a victim in Garrett's sick game, which is why I led Val to believe that Sam knew that she was coming.

In my defense, I didn't actually say yes when Val asked me. I didn't say no, either. Instead, I casually changed the subject, hoping that she wouldn't ask again.

Everything is so screwed up.

On the bright side, Dad has been here on weekends as he promised to check on things. His visits do nothing for my sloppy reasoning, but him being here does manage to lift my spirits for a moment in time. He's proud of me for the way things are going so far, and I enjoy the work I'm doing.

I've spent far more than a couple of hours at the office. Work has been my escape lately, a way to keep my mind off of my real problems.

I've only spoken to Sam three times since I left. Each call has been short and awkward. I've made it a point to call her right before she goes to work, just enough time for only the important words that need to be heard.

I miss you.

I wish you were here.

I love you.

I'm afraid that if the call lasts any longer, she'll ask me about my day, which in turn could lead to my unspoken truth.

Regardless of how messed up things are, I can't lose her.

Not now.

Not ever.

I'm going to tell her about Val when I get home when she's able to look me in my eyes and hopefully understand my intent. I can't fathom the thought that she may put me in the same category as Garrett. It's time to get over myself and make things right with Sam.

"Knock, knock." Val raps on the inside of the door frame before entering the office. She plops down into the chair before me, stealing my attention away from the unending traffic outside.

I lean back in my chair, giving her a boyish grin.

"Is everything okay? You seem different today." Her head slants to the right. Her stare reaches for a truth that I won't admit to, not all of it.

"I'm fine. Just thinking about Sam." I blow out a long breath.

"You miss her." Val acknowledges as a fact.

It's hard to believe that years ago, she was the only girl on my mind. I never would've surmised that we would be here together talking about a relationship with someone that I'm in love with. I'd sworn off love for this very reason. I didn't want all of the drama. I didn't want to be hurt. I never wanted to be in a position to hurt someone else the way my parents were hurt.

"I do." I lean forward to rest my arms on the desk. My heart grows tired with every moment we spend apart.

Val eyes me warily, reading me from the outside in. "So, what are you going to do about it?"

Val's words sting me, making me question why I ever left without Sam. I know my reasoning. She had to work. Her life doesn't stop just because I pick up and leave at a moment's notice. But still, I wish she were here with me. I haven't been without her for this long since we met.

"We're much further ahead of schedule here than we anticipated." Val leans forward and touches her hand to mine on the desk. "We should be finished in the next few days if we stay focused. Maybe your father will agree to shorten our visit."

"I think that can be arranged."

We both jump at the sound of my dad's voice echoing across the office. Val jerks her hand away from mine, standing abruptly.

"Mr. Pierce." Val greets dad carefully.

"Dad. I didn't notice you standing there." I scoot my chair away from the desk to stand.

"I don't see a reason to keep you here longer than needed if the job is done," he says, looking between the two of us.

I sense that he wants to say more, but he doesn't. I'm sure our reactions made the scene appear more intimate than it was. Neither one of us responds.

"Then it's settled." Dad claps his hand together once. "I'll stay a few more days and help you finish up, pending approval from your mother." He chuckles. "You've both done well. I'm taking you out to celebrate tonight."

Val opens her mouth to say something but decides against it. I imagine she doesn't know what to make of our relationship. When she left, dad and I weren't on the best of speaking terms. He was practically a stranger to me because of my foolish pride.

"Unless you two have other plans," Dad says accusingly.

"No, sir," Val spits out. "I would love to go."

"Son?" Dad asks.

"Sure. I could use a decent meal." My diet has consisted of sandwiches and junk food since I got here. Val refused to go to dinner with me, and I didn't see the point in going alone.

"I've scoped out a nice place not too far from the hotel. You kids head out and get freshened up. Let's meet in the lobby around seven, and I'll drive us."

"Sounds like a plan, Mr. Pierce," Val says.

All I can do is nod my agreement. My mind is still very much on Sam, but dinner may be just the thing that I need to distract me.

Val stops by my room on her way to the lobby, twenty minutes early. She's always been a stickler for time.

"Hi." She chirps when I open the door.

"Hey. Come on in. I'm not quite ready yet. I was about to jump in the shower." I scratch the back of my neck while she looks around nervously.

She's still as beautiful as ever, and I'd be a fool not to notice. I flip the hair hanging over her shoulder through my fingers. This is the first time I've seen her relaxed since this ordeal began.

"You let your hair down tonight. Hot date?" I ask.

"Not a chance. Though, I do hope to have one when I return home. You kind of ruined my first one." She gives me a teasing smile.

I force a smile, grunting at her statement. Visions of her and Garrett together flash through my mind. I want to tell her who he really is, but I can't betray Sam's trust. I'll have to find another way to keep her away from him. For now, avoidance seems like the best course of action.

Val tilts her head to the side, gauging my reaction. "Uh-oh. I know that look. Something is bothering you. Is it the thought of me on a date with some other guy?" she asks.

I don't care who she spends her time with. It's none of my business. We've both moved on a long time ago. I just don't like the idea of her being with this guy. I don't want to see her get hurt.

"I only want to see you happy." *And Garrett is not the guy to make that happen,* I think to myself.

We stand in awkward silence for a moment longer staring into each other's eyes, before Val looks away. The connection between us is still so thick. Both of us seek comfort and assurance, yet we're cautious not to cross the line.

I clear my throat and begin to back away. "I should go get ready. We don't want to keep dad waiting. I'll be right back."

Chapter 2

Samantha

Somewhere in the back of my mind, I thought things would have gotten easier by now. I imagined that Brad and I would both forget what happened and move on. Our reality couldn't be further from it. Brad jumped at the first chance he had to get away from the mess I made, and I pretended that I was okay with it. I let him believe that distance was not a problem.

We keep in touch, but we haven't really talked about much during our short phone conversations. I try not to read too much into Brad's impeccable timing when he calls me right before I leave for work. I want to believe that he's not hiding. I want to believe that his love for me is equally as strong as before. So, I don't push. I don't question. I'm giving him the space he needs, and maybe it will be enough. Maybe this space, without me in it, will bring all of him back to me.

I've taken a couple of extra shifts at work this week, and I make it a point to avoid the busy hours of the day if I need to go out for something, until today. As much as I loathe the idea of running into Garrett, I'd rather not make an extra trip to the store just for milk tonight.

I enter the store with one thing on my mind, getting the one item that I came for and leaving. I head in the direction of the freezers quickly, careful not to make eye contact with anyone. I don't want to be deterred from my mission.

I reach inside for a half-gallon of milk and nearly drop it when I turn and find Garrett at the other end of the aisle. I suck in a sharp breath at the sight of him. He smiles when he sees me as if nothing ever happened. I'm slightly thrown off by it, sick even.

Does he not remember what he did to me, how he violated me, and ruined any chances of us ever being cordial again? The smirk on his face says that he doesn't care.

In my mind, I turn and run away out of fright, scared of what he may have planned next, but my feet fail me. I can't move. I want to scream for someone to come and help me as he begins to walk toward me, but I know that it would be pointless. It would only fuel him further.

So, I wait, forcing my breath to calm.

And wait...

The closer he gets, the more my fear turns to anger and resentment. His once sexy walk is not so sexy anymore. Every step he takes prickles my skin in the worst way. I could walk away. I should walk away, but my curiosity gets the best of me.

He stops a few inches away from me, and I wait for him to speak. I stare into those eyes that I loved so much.

"Samantha." He says my name with such care, without apology or regret.

"Garrett." I force myself to speak, refusing to back down from whatever game this is he's playing.

"It's funny running into you here of all places."

I give him a curt smile. "I was just thinking the same thing. If I didn't know any better, I'd say you were following me." I look down at his empty hands for emphasis. "I have an excuse for being here," I say as I tap the carton in my hand. "What's yours?"

He steps closer causing my breath to hitch. It's so wrong, the way I'm feeling right now. I'm furious, but at the same time, I remember how it felt that night. I remember every touch and every kiss, every whisper, and every command. I loved the way he made me feel, and I hate him for it. I brace myself for his next move.

He tilts his head and moves in even closer. My eyes close at the warmth of his breath rolling over my cheeks. I unwillingly breathe in his masculine scent.

"Babe, I'm flattered that you'd think I'm following you."

I feel the slightest touch from his lips to my earlobe. Then it quickly fades.

"Now, if you'll excuse me," he says, stepping around me. "I need to get going."

He stops in front of the whipped cream and picks up a can. He glances at me and smiles, this time more cunning. His tongue slinks out of his mouth in a slow taunting motion, causing my body to react before he turns and walks away, leaving me standing with my mouth hanging open.

I hate him because he still has the power to make me feel something for him. He has the power to awaken forbidden thoughts. He has the power to do as he pleases while I silently suffer inside.

I hate him because I once loved him. I fear that our past is keeping me from doing what's right for my future.

When I get home, I forgot why I needed milk in the first place. I'm not in the mood to eat anything. My thoughts are consumed with him, and I've finally had enough. The only way to get him off of my mind is to replace him with someone else, the one I should be thinking about.

I pull out my phone and stare at it for a minute, contemplating if I should. I haven't called Brad once since he left. He's always been the initiator. It's after hours and close enough to the time he usually calls. I eye his name for a few seconds more before I click on the green symbol. I just want to hear his voice. I need him to assure me that he's still in this with me.

"Hello." A familiar voice meets my ears through the receiver, but it's not Brad's voice that I hear. It's Valerie.

"Valerie?" I ask, confused. I force myself not to jump to conclusions.

"Yes." She says a little too cheery.

"I was trying to reach Brad. Is he there with you?"

"Yes, he's in the shower. I saw it…"

I cut her off, not wanting to hear another word. I can't deal with this right now. "I'll call back later," I say in a rush. I end the call and fall back onto the couch.

As if I didn't already have enough on my plate. Brad's supposed to be on a business trip. Why would she be answering his phone? Did he lie to me about going so that he could spend time with her? Maybe Brad was her reason for returning after all, and she received her wish.

I want to believe in Brad, but he's been acting so strange lately. I want to believe that there's a perfectly good explanation for all of this. I have to believe it, or I'll go insane with worry, but I don't want to hear it from her. He has to be the one to either break or ease my aching heart.

Chapter 3

Bradley

Val told me that Sam called while I was in the shower. She didn't understand why Sam hung up the phone before she could get a word in. I mentally punch myself for leaving my phone unattended. I can't be upset with Val because I didn't exactly tell her the whole truth either.

This isn't the way I wanted Sam to find out about Val. She probably thinks I'm the worst person in the world. I feel like the worst for keeping this from her.

In a panic, I try to call her back, but she doesn't answer. So, I send her a quick text.

Brad: Hey, Sam. Sorry I missed your call. I never meant for you to find out like this. We need to talk. I will explain everything. I promise.

I hit send without giving it much thought. I fail to tell Sam that I love her. If dad weren't waiting for us to show up, I'd ditch dinner and go home to her. I can only imagine what she must be thinking.

"Is everything alright, Bradley?"

I look over at Val standing across the room. I hate lying to her. I hate lying to either of them. I force a smile to try and ward off any further inquisition. I don't know how much longer I can keep this up.

"She didn't answer, but I'm sure everything's fine. It's just our usual nightly call, nothing out of the ordinary." Except it is. It's not like Sam to call me. "I'll try again after dinner."

Val's questioning stare stirs me. I begin to wonder if things truly are okay. I turn to face her and slip the phone into my pocket.

"How did she seem when you spoke to her? Did she sound okay?" I ask Val.

"Other than her sudden hangup?" Val asks. "She sounded confused and surprised."

I close my eyes for a few seconds. I have a lot of explaining to do when I see her. This is a conversation best had when face to face.

A soft touch on my arm brings me back to the present. Val stands next to me with a worried expression, but she doesn't ask the questions that I know are on the tip of her tongue, and I don't answer with the words on the tip of mine. It's not my story to tell, not until I speak with Sam about it first.

We're both equally as stubborn as the other. Val is usually the one to give in and say what's on her mind, but something holds her back now. Maybe it's the look in my eyes that warns her against pushing.

"If you need to talk, Bradley, I'm here." She offers me a sad smile. Her eyes tell me how much she wants to help, but can't because I won't allow it.

Even if I did let her in, she can't fix what's broken. She can't take back what's already been done.

"I know you are." I return her smile. "We need to go before dad comes calling."

"You're right," she says, pulling her hand away. "Your dad is kind of scary. I wouldn't want to be caught with my hands all over you twice in one day," she says with a tiny chuckle.

I wiggle my brows playfully. "Are you sure about that?"

Val purses her lips and taps her finger to her chin. "Uhm, I'm pretty sure. You're a kept man now. We can't have anything messing that up, right?"

"Right," I say in response.

Val walks toward the door and glances back over her shoulder. "I would tell you if Samantha wasn't right for you. I might have even tried to steal you away, but I like her, and she loves you. Anyone can see it."

She reaches the door and pauses before opening it. There's something hidden in her eyes that I can't touch, something that she doesn't want me to see. She places her hand on my right cheek. Her touch is soothing, but it's not her touch that I long for. It makes me miss Sam even more.

"She's lucky to have you, Bradley. You're lucky to have each other." She takes a small pause. "If, and I say this without possibility… If I were to ever consider falling in love, I'd want to have a love like yours. I don't think I'll ever surpass what we had ever again."

She smiles sadly, then opens the door and walks away. I don't know what to say to her. I don't know how to feel.

Val has never said anything like that to me before. I've always believed that we were on the same page when we were younger. Neither one of us wanted to fall in love. I loved her, and she loved me, but we didn't want the fairytale. There were no expectations, no possibility of a future together. We were two teenagers with a shared reality, guarding our hearts against a cruel world. What she just revealed sounds quite the opposite.

For her to do this now, it seems cruel. She knows that I won't question her because I'm a good guy, and my heart belongs to someone else.

I shake off the inquiry about what just happened. I won't be that guy. I will not live in the past when I have so much to look forward to. Sam is my reality, and even though our lives are slightly tilted right now, she is my future. Whatever could have become of Val and me was lost the day that she left. There is no reason to question it.

Neither one of us says a word in the elevator. We both hurry out the moment the doors open. Dad's car is parked curbside when we get downstairs. Val opts for the back seat, and I sit up front with dad. It's one of the most awkward rides I've ever had. I can feel her eyes on me the entire time.

I'm thankful that the restaurant wasn't far away when we arrive. I don't think I could take Val's scorching eyes against my skin any longer. During dinner, I eat while dad quizzes Val about herself. I'm tuned out for the most part.

"I have some good news," Dad says over dessert. "I've hired an interim manager until I can find someone more permanent."

Dad's statement grabs my attention. I wonder when he had time to find a manager.

"I know what you're thinking." He chuckles. "I spoke with one of the guys currently on-site, Chuck. I've been watching all of the guys the past couple of weeks. Chuck seems like the best fit. He knows how everything is supposed to work, and the other guys respect him."

"Good choice," I say with a nod. I like Chuck. He has a good head on his shoulders, but something about my dad's decision stings me. I know he said Chuck is temporary, but he's still looking for someone else. He didn't think to ask me if I wanted the job, even though I don't know if I would take it. I have Sam to consider. My life is in Lakin, but it would've meant the world to me if he'd thought of me first. "I have someone in mind to take the position permanently. I just haven't gotten around to asking." Dad gives me an intense look as if he's expecting me to say more or ask who, but I stay quiet. "I can handle the books from home until then. Now that set up is done, Chuck should be able to handle everything else once we leave for home tomorrow."

I perk up at the mention of going home. There is so much that I want to say to Sam. "Tomorrow?" I ask, to be sure.

"Yes. I think it's time." Dad looks between Val and me. "You could both use the break," he says meaningfully.

He didn't blurt it out, but I can read between the lines perfectly. He thinks that Val and I are a little too close for comfort. If anyone knows the signs that lead to destruction, it's him. He's lived through it. I'm beginning to think that his thinking is right.

Chapter 4

Samantha

I took a long shower to try and wash away some of my insecurities. I think it's safe to say that I failed miserably. It's almost comical. It's a situation I would laugh about if I were on the tail end of it, but not knowing how things will turn out holds me back.

I believe everyone is entitled to feel a little insecure every so often, but my levels have risen to an unhealthy degree after that phone call. I stare at my naked body in the mirror, taking note of all of my flaws. I wonder if Brad ever noticed them. I imagine that Val doesn't have many. She's practically perfect.

I sigh heavily at the sound of my phone ringing for the second time tonight. I'm not in the mood to talk to on the phone. I miss him. I want him here with me. Only then can I move past my loneliness and hear what he has to say.

I wrap a towel around me and walk over to my phone lying on the bed. I look down at the screen, and my heart picks up a few beats.

Robert?

I wrinkle my forehead in confusion. Why would Robert be calling me?

Unless…

Lacy!

My first thought is that something happened to Lacy. My second thought is the baby. Will I have to mourn for both of them, or is it my turn to be strong for Lacy? I can't fathom the thought of either of those things at this point. I don't want to lose them.

I cover my mouth with my hand at the thought. I pick the phone up with my other hand and stare at it hard, afraid to answer. My thumb hovers over the screen until it stops ringing. It's my second cowardly act of the day.

I don't like confrontation when the outcome seems grim, which is why I didn't want to hear what Valerie had to say. It's the same reason I have for not picking up the phone when Robert called. My life is full of confusion and uncertainty right now. I want to know what's happening, but I'm afraid to find out.

I jump at the feel of my phone vibrating in my hand. The ring is drowned out by my morbid thoughts. I force my thumb down onto the screen and bring the phone up to my ear.

"Hello," I say cautiously.

"Hi, Samantha. It's me, Robert." He pauses on the other end of the line. There is a calmness in his voice, but his words are whispered. Even so, my heart still beats frantically.

"Is everything okay? Lacy? The baby?" I manage to ask without sounding out my feelings.

"Yes. Yes. Lacy and the baby are both fine. I'm calling because I wanted to invite you to Lacy's baby shower tomorrow."

I release the breath I'd been holding and sit down on the bed.

"My parents moved the date up so that we could surprise her. I know it's short notice, but it would mean the world to her if you could make it. I thought about waiting another week, but it's hard to plan a surprise when she's always with me. I'm not the best at keeping secrets from her. She knows me so well. It will only take one day before she recognizes that I'm keeping something from her and pries it out of me." Robert laughs.

His laugh makes me laugh. I think it's the first time that I've felt anything remotely close to happiness in the past two weeks since Brad has been gone. It feels good.

"Samantha?" Robert asks.

"Yes. I'm here. Of course I'll be there. I wouldn't miss it for anything."

"Good." He sighs loudly into the phone.

"Should I bring something? Do you need help with anything?" I think it's sweet that he's doing this for Lacy. I would've done it eventually, but with everything going on, it would've been later rather than sooner.

"No. Everything is already planned. My parents took care of everything with your dad's help. We all agreed to have it at his house. That way, Lacy has no clue what's about to happen."

"Great!" I say cheerfully. I pause for a second, thinking about my next words. "Robert?" I question.

"Yes?"

"How is she? How is the baby?" I ask him with a hint of concern in my voice. Robert and I don't talk much, but I figure this is as good of an excuse as any to spark up a conversation.

"They're great. Other than a little discomfort when Lacy sleeps, she's fine. They're perfect."

I'm relieved to hear that. I can hear the adoration in Robert's voice. He has always treated Lacy with the utmost respect. There was never any question about what he feels for her, and by the sound of it, his heart has already made room for one more.

Their reality makes me think about my reality and how I wish things could go back to the way they were. I'm still smiling, but I don't realize that I'm also crying until a tear slides down my face.

"I can't wait to see them." I wipe the tears of confusion away from my face.

"She misses you. She'll be glad to see you."

My eyes well up at his words. Lacy can't possibly miss me more than I miss her.

After I end the call with Robert, I contemplate calling Brad. It will be two whole weeks before he's back home.

Two more weeks of sleeping alone.

Eating alone.

Waking up alone.

Being alone.

I walk around our apartment full of things, but the air feels just as hollow as my heart. The only good thing that I have to look forward to is the baby shower tomorrow. I'm supposed to be working tomorrow, but my manager knew I was on standby if anything happened with my sister.

I consider this an emergency.

I scroll through my contacts and call Viv. She answers on the third ring.

"Hey, honey. It must be important if you're calling me at this time of night," she says with a laugh.

Viv gave me her number to use for emergencies when I first started working alongside her. I only remember using it once when I got stuck in traffic on my way to work.

"Hi, Viv. I'm sorry to call so late."

"Oh, shush. I was only going over the menu for tomorrow. What's up?"

"Would it be terrible if I were to skip work tomorrow? My family has a surprise baby shower planned for my sister, and I would hate to miss it." I pout into the phone as if she can somehow see me.

"Absolutely," she responds immediately.

"Wait. Absolutely? As in absolutely, it would be terrible or absolutely take the day off?" I ask. I'm really hoping it's the latter. It will give me three days off to spend with my family.

"I'll be fine. Go. Enjoy yourself. You can make it up to me later. And tell that sexy young thang of yours I said hello."

My laugh reverberates through the apartment. Almost everything out of Viv's mouth makes me laugh. She has made her thoughts about Brad's looks clear from the moment I introduced them. I only laugh because I know she's harmless.

"I will. Your comment is sure to make Brad blush."

When I hang up from Viv, I look around the apartment again. It's still full of stuff. I'm still alone.

My mind isn't ready to shut down for the night, and I'm not tired in the least. It's only a few hours drive to my dad's. So, I get dressed, pack my bags, and leave.

Chapter 5

Bradley

I'm up before sunrise the next morning. I barely slept thinking about what I want to say to Sam and how she will react to my words. I thought about how wrong I was for not telling her. I wonder if what I've done has pushed me over the line.

Even in my small stretch of sleep, I dreamt of her. I dreamt of us together, happy, and in love. I also had a nightmare that jarred me awake and has me packing my bags at four in the morning. The images of her and Garrett walking hand-in-hand continue to play in my mind. In my slumber, I reached for her to no avail. They walked past me like I was invisible. They stopped just out of my reach, and she turned to face him. He bent to meet her waiting lips. I tried hard to move, to stop it from happening. The more I struggled to get to her, the more her knees weakened under his control. I stood helpless as he took what was mine. When it was over, he wrapped his arm around her shoulder and leaned in close to kiss her temple. They were happy. I was furious, but there was nothing that I could do about it.

This time away from Sam has made me appreciate her so much more. I love her more now than yesterday and the day before. Me waking up in a pool of sweat confirmed as much. I have to do something to piece us back together before it's too late.

I send dad a text message and write a quick note for Val. I stop at her room door and raise my fist to knock but think better of it. I lower my arm and place my forehead against the cold wood thinking. *Things would be so much easier if she hadn't said what she did.* I hope she understands why I'm leaving without saying goodbye. After last night, I think it's a must that I give her some space.

The ride home appears to be much longer than I remember from before. It's only me, the open road, and my wayward thoughts. I think until it becomes overwhelming.

I turn on the music and try to get into it. I try singing until I began to laugh at how ridiculous I sound. Sam would get a kick out of this.

When I finally make it home, my first instinct is to rush to her side, pull her to me, and kiss her so intense that it will melt her from the inside out. I would love nothing more than to pretend that there isn't a crack in our foundation, but I can't. I remember how I left, why I left, and what I almost did to her in my rage.

I exit the car, grab my bags, and walk at an even pace toward the front door. I pause for a few seconds before going inside. I walk quietly down the hallway in case she's still asleep. I drop my bags by the bedroom door and stop when I don't see her. The bed's not made, but I don't hear any noise in the bathroom.

"Sam," I call through the apartment. I check every room in the apartment before calling out again. "Sam. I'm home. Where are you?"

No answer.

I check the closet, notice her bag missing, and immediately think the worst. "Fuck." I feel like I'm back in that parking lot listening to Garrett tell me his dirty little secret. I feel like I'm losing her all over again.

I pull out my phone and call her, but it goes straight to voicemail.

"Hi, Samantha here. Leave a message."

"Hey, Sam. It's me. I came home early. I wanted to surprise you, but I guess the jokes on me, huh? I get that you don't want to talk. Just let me know that you're okay. I love you."

I hang on for a few seconds before I end the call. I sit down on the sofa to piece together my thoughts.

Where could she be? Why didn't she tell me she was leaving? Is she coming back? So many valid questions that I wish I didn't have to think about.

"Please come back home, Sam," I whisper. "I don't want to do this without you."

I was going stir crazy waiting for a call or text or anything from Sam. It never came. So, I called Nate. He suggested that we get a few games in at the pool bar and assured me that Garrett would not be around, stating that he left for a couple of days to meet with a pro team.

I'm stoked that he's gone, but my mind immediately went to Sam when I heard the news. I would feel much better if I knew that Garrett went alone. I convince myself that it's just a coincidence. She wouldn't.

I step into the pool bar around noon to meet up with Nate. He has the table set and ready for play when I walk inside. I recall the last time that I was here. When Garrett told me he understood that Sam was off-limits.

"Hey, man." Nate slaps his hand against my shoulder to get my attention.

I hadn't realized I'd stopped and was staring at the back wall.

"Hey. Good to see you." I say to Nate.

"You sure you're up for this?" He asks.

I laugh at his question. Even if I wasn't, I'm here now. I nod my head toward the table. "Since the moment you talked me into it," I reply smartly.

We pick out a pool stick and toss a coin to see who goes first. Nate chalks his cue and leans down to get into position.

He looks up at me before he shoots to spout off a witty comment.

"Prepare to get your ass kicked."

"Don't be too sure about that," I reply.

Nate shoots and sinks it, over and over and over again, until my solid balls are all that's left, minus the two that I managed to sink in between.

I don't care that I've lost the game. I'm thankful that I was able to clear my mind for a while and hang out with my friend.

"I'll go grab us a couple of drinks," Nate says. "You want anything else?" He asks as he backs away.

"A cheeseburger would be nice," I reply.

"Snag us a table, and I'll meet you there."

I look around for an empty table and find one on the upper level. I get Nate's attention and point in that direction. He nods, letting me know that he understands. I sit and observe people moving about doing all of the things that I miss. Talking. Dancing. Kissing. I even miss something as simple as a playful conversation.

"Large crowd this evening." Nate places the tray of food down on the table and sits across from me.

"I agree. You couldn't have picked a better time," I say sarcastically. I take a bottle from the tray and take a swig.

"Anything to help out a damsel in distress." He says with a cheeky grin.

I laugh outwardly at his misguided humor. "Damsel, huh?"

"Yeah." He tilts his bottle in my direction in an air toast.

"Did I hear someone say, Damsel?"

We turn towards the interruption. I glance at Nate and wrinkle my forehead in confusion, wondering if he knows the two girls standing at our table. His demeanor remains relaxed as he stares at the girl that spoke. I notice the corner of his mouth turns up into a smile. He takes a drink from his bottle and places it on the table, grabs the girl by her waist, and pulls her onto his lap.

"You are hardly a Damsel," he says to her. He pushes a few loose strands of hair behind her ear and leans in to whisper something in her ear that makes her giggle.

The other girl stands patiently waiting for whatever they're doing to be over.

I take another drink and set my bottle down with my hand still wrapped around it. "Aren't you going to introduce me to your friend?" I ask Nate.

"I wasn't planning on it," Nate says without looking at me.

His mystery girl smacks his arm playfully and swivels on his lap to face me. Her hand juts out in my direction.

"He's being silly. I'm Kelly, and this is my friend Brenda," she says, nodding to the other girl. "Nice to meet you."

I shake her hand and glance at Nate. He chuckles behind her.

"So, are you two....?" My question hangs in the air. Nate didn't have a girlfriend when I left a few weeks ago, but things can change in the blink of an eye.

"Me and Nate?" She asks. "No." She exaggerates. "We're just..." She pauses for a split second. "...good friends. I scratch his itch, and he scratches mine."

I study her for a moment. I don't buy her story one bit. Nate may be on board with this, but she's definitely not. She's more into him than she's saying. Her explanation

37

would have been believable if I hadn't seen that small hint of sadness in her expression when she said it.

    We sit in awkward silence for a moment. Then Kelly suddenly stands.

    "I didn't mean to interrupt." She says. "I mean, I did but…," she snickers and gives Nate her full attention. "Can I steal you away for a minute?"

    He looks at me as if to ask for my approval. I shrug like it's no big deal. Kelly tugs at his arm until he stands, and they leave me here with her friend without another word. I guess it's up to me to invite her to sit, to engage in friendly conversation even if it's the last thing that I want to do with a complete stranger tonight.

    "That was…" I pause to choose my next word wisely. I don't want to come off as a jerk by stating the obvious. Her friend was inconsiderate for bailing on her the way she did. "…strange of her to leave you standing here without an explanation. Would you like to sit?" I ask.

    "Sure," she replies. "We all have that one friend, right?" She jokes, taking Nate's seat across from me.

    I think about my friends and nod in agreement. One, in particular, comes to mind. I know exactly what she means.

The type of friend that's not satisfied unless the world revolves around them. The type of friend that won't think twice about hurting the people they claim to love to get what they want.

I lift my bottle and take another drink. Nate and his special friend are on the dance floor swaying to the music. I try to avoid eye contact with Brenda at all costs. I don't want her to get the wrong impression. She must notice because she tries to spark up a conversation.

"Do you come here often? I've never seen you around."

Brenda looks nervous, unlike Kelly, who seems far from timid. She doesn't want to be in this position any more than I do. Her hands are in her lap underneath the table. I notice the gentle shake of her shoulders, probably from her legs bouncing.

"Only when I'm convinced by a good friend that it's a good idea," I say, nodding towards the dance floor.

She smiles. "Would you like to-to dance?" She stutters.

I seem to be on a roll lately, breaking hearts. Why stop now? "I don't think my girl would take too kindly to that."

"It's just a dance." She mumbles under her breath, surprising herself. She covers her mouth and looks away when she realizes that I'd heard her.

"It's just a dance," I repeat. "Until it's not."

"I'm sorry. I wasn't trying to…"

I hold my hand up, halting her explanation. "Don't worry about it." I drink what's left in my bottle and send Nate a message. He's so wrapped up in Kelly. He likely won't see it until later. I eye the burger in front of me. My appetite is nonexistent now. "I shouldn't be here."

What I want to say is I shouldn't be here with you. It should be Sam sitting across from me. She should be the one I'm having a conversation with. And she would be if I knew where the hell she was.

I stand, say goodbye to Brenda, and leave.

Chapter 6

Samantha

I snuck in while dad was asleep last night and crashed right away from the long drive. I woke up early this morning to make breakfast, deciding it was the best way to make my presence known.

I'm still not feeling my best, but I haven't felt this good in a while. Being back home has that effect on me. I feel safe and protected as if nothing can harm me here. I can clear my mind of what's broken, if only for a little while.

I didn't bother returning Brad's call after listening to his message. Though I did listen to the message over and over again just to hear his voice. He sounded sincere enough. I miss him. I miss him so much it hurts.

"How's my Sammy doing this morning."

I smile at Dad's familiar calling. I didn't realize how much I've missed it until now. Somehow, hearing his voice grants me permission to release some of the bad that I'd been holding in. I blow out a long breath and turn to face him.

I rush to him, and he gives me one of his signature bear hugs. "Sammy is doing just fine, Dad. I've missed you." I add to the script. I keep my arms wrapped around his neck a little too long before I finally release him. "How are you?"

He stares at me. He knows that Lacy is the reason that I came, but he also knows me. He senses that something is wrong, and his Sammy is not just fine.

"More importantly, how are you? Truthfully," Dad says with a hint of concern.

I don't want to explain to my dad that my ex betrayed me again, or that Brad's been away for more than two weeks and another woman answered his phone. I also don't want to lie to him.

Knowing that he would never pressure me, I say, "Is it okay if I don't want to talk about it? This is Lacy's day. I'd like to focus on her."

"If that's what you want. Just know that I'm here if you need me."

I recognize that it pains him to see me hurting, and even more that I won't let him try to help. "I know dad, and I love you for it."

He draws in a deep breath, closes his eyes, and opens them slowly on exhale. "Mmm. Breakfast." He says, changing the subject as if he's just entered the kitchen.

"I cooked," I say proudly. "I didn't want you to wake up and think a stranger was in the house."

"One of your finest ideas. You turned over two stones at once."

"I guess I did. Are you hungry?"

He gives me a stern but playful look. "You don't even have to ask. I wouldn't say no, even if I weren't."

Over breakfast, dad catches me up on things that I've missed since I've been gone. It's everything that I'd expected to hear except the part about him dating. I'm sure he's socialized with women before and probably a few other things that I'd rather not discuss with him. It would be crazy if he hadn't throughout the years. He's just never spelled it out so clearly to me before. I'm happy for him. He deserves to be happy.

"So, who's the lucky lady?" I ask after finishing off the last of my breakfast.

"Her name is Margaret. You'll meet her today at the baby shower."

My brows raise slightly in shock. "That serious, huh?"

Dad leans back in his chair and pats his hands against his full belly. "It's only been a few months, but we've gotten pretty close. I think it's time she met my two favorite girls."

I smile at his sentiment.

"I don't think that I'll ever feel again what I felt with your mother, but I do love Margaret, and she loves me. I have no doubt that she is the next best thing for me."

"Does Lacy know?" I ask.

"She does. It will be the first time that she's met her, though. I wanted to wait until I was sure before I introduced you." Dad studies me closely.

I watch him for a moment. Though there's a sadness in his words, I recognize the look, the dreamy eyes, the boyish smile, and the hope that what once was lost can be found again.

"I can't wait to meet her," I say.

Everyone parked their cars either behind or away from the house so as not to alarm Lacy when she arrives. Her biggest surprise showed up about fifteen minutes ago. This one even shocked me. It was definitely unexpected for sure, and all thanks to Robert and Dad.

"Shh, everyone quiet down. They just pulled up," dad announces from the front window.

The plan is that Robert and Lacy are coming over to check on dad as usual. When she walks in, we'll all yell surprise and pray that she doesn't go into early labor.

Dad counts down from three with his fingers held high in the air, letting us know to get ready. They're approaching the door. My stomach flutters in anticipation. The air is sucked out of the room as everyone draws in a breath. The keys jiggle in the lock, and when the door opens, we all yell, "Surprise!"

Lacy freezes in the doorway. Her hand covers her belly protectively. I hold my breath right along with her and don't let it go until she does. Robert grasps her waist to hold her steady. Her eyes roam across the room at all of the familiar faces; me, dad, Mr. & Mrs. Thomas, Grandma Ann & Grandpa Dave, and a few of her co-workers. Lacy begins to cry when her eyes land on Grandma Liz & Grandpa Carl, who appear to be on the verge of tears.

Dad and Robert managed to keep that secret from both of us. I had no idea they would be here. I'd already made up my mind that Lacy and I would visit them before I left. Now we don't have to.

"You guys," she whines through her tears. "You didn't have to…" She looks up at Robert, who's grinning widely. "How did you manage to keep this from me?" She sniffles. Robert places a quick peck on her cheek.

"Trust me. It wasn't easy," Robert tells Lacy.

"And you." Lacy's eyes land on me.

I shrug. I don't feel guilty at all about keeping this secret. The look on Lacy's face was priceless.

"We finally managed to pull one over your head," I say to her.

My comment breaks the silence in the room and gains quite a few agreements.

After Lacy settles down and stops crying, the shower begins. We play a few games, and Robert surprises me with his willing participation. He actually let us blindfold him and feed him random baby food. I have it all on camera.

We play more games. We eat. We talk. Baby Thomas is bringing us all closer together. Everything is falling into place. Everything except my personal life.

Chapter 7

Bradley

This is either the best or the worst decision that I've ever made. I can't decide yet. I had every intention of going home when I left the bar. Instead of sticking with the plan, I followed my gut.

I called ahead and booked me a hotel room, but I didn't go straight there to check-in. I still haven't heard from Sam. I tried calling. Once, when I left the bar and again while I was driving. Each time I was met by her sweet voice telling me to leave a message, and both times I did.

I have a habit of sitting in cars in front of people's houses. I've been here for over an hour. Waiting. Watching people slowly trickle out to leave.

I was about to call off my impromptu mission when I finally catch a glimpse of her through the open door. *My Sam.* It only lasts for a few seconds before the door closes, and I'm shut out again. Seeing her here gives me permission to breathe freely. It takes away the doubt that I had earlier.

I gaze at my riding companions that I picked up on the way here. I don't know how she'll react to me being here, but I have to try.

By the time I make it to the door, my nerves begin to kick in. I have no qualms about being here. I don't feel bad about interrupting what looks like a family function. I only hope that Sam doesn't send me away.

I ring the doorbell and knock for added coverage. I can only imagine what I must look like to the neighbors with one hand behind my back standing here.

I was hoping that it would be Sam staring back at me when the door swings open, but it isn't. Her dad answers, and I can't decipher if he's happy to see me or pissed by my sudden appearance. His expression only gives away one emotion. Confused. He definitely didn't expect me to show up at his door.

"Bradley. Sammy didn't tell me you were coming." His forehead wrinkles, but he quickly corrects it.

What did Sam tell him? Does he know what happened?

"I'm sorry for the intrusion Mr. Young." How do I explain my presence here without telling a lie, without knowing how much he knows? "I was worried about Sam. She wasn't answering her phone." It's the perfect excuse, and all of it true.

"Don't be sorry. Come in. I'll get Sammy for you."

I breathe a sigh of relief. Mr. Young steps aside for me to enter and closes the door behind us.

"Sammy." He yells above the chaos.

"Yes, Dad?" Sam's voice echoes from down the hall.

"You have a visitor." Her dad says in response. He turns to me. "Make yourself at home Bradley. Would you like a drink? Something to...."

His words fade into the background when I spot Sam walking towards me. Her expression was much like her dad's when he opened the door. Only with Sam, the hurt peeks through. I hate knowing that I've caused her pain.

Her steps pause for a few seconds when she looks up and realizes that I'm her infamous guest. She swallows hard and brushes her hands across her thighs. I hold my breath as she approaches. I study her, hanging on to her every move. Luscious body that I long to touch. Soft hair that I haven't been able to run my fingers through. Eyes that haven't seen mine in weeks. And finally, lips that I need to kiss. "Brad, I wasn't expecting you." She says, dismantling my daydream. She obviously doesn't feel the way that I do. *Who were you expecting?* I want to ask but don't. Instead, I say. "I know. I tried calling, but…" I stop and look around. Everyone is quiet now, watching us like we're the main attraction. "Can we go somewhere and talk?" I ask her.

She looks at her dad. He watches her for any sign that she may want him to kick me out. She smiles and looks back at me. "Follow me," she says.

It's hard to know what she's thinking. Sam begins to walk back toward the hallway, and I have no choice but to follow. The noise picks up when we exit. I feel like I'm being led into the lion's den. It might have been safer if we had gone outside. Then I wouldn't have to do the walk of shame when she tells me it's over.

I'm sure the sound of the door closing behind me is exaggerated by my thoughts. "These are for you." I held out six, short-stemmed sunflowers and handed them to her. I thought I saw a hint of a smile, but I can't be sure. It was gone almost as soon as it appeared. It seems silly now. Who brings a girl sunflowers? I'd gotten them to remind her that she's still my yellow.

"Thanks. They're beautiful." She brings them to her nose and sniffs. "Should I put them in water?" She asks.

As bad as I want to touch her, I stuff my hands in my pockets to keep from doing so. "I think so. Honestly, I don't really know. They reminded me of you. And so…" I shrug.

She looks around the room for something she can't seem to find. Then, she goes into the bathroom, runs water into the sink, and places them inside. She stops a few feet away from me when she steps back into the room.

"Sam, I…"

"Brad, I…"

We speak simultaneously.

"You go first," she says.

I hadn't thought about what I would say to her or how I would explain. I just knew it had to be done now.

"I don't know where to start," I say truthfully.

"You could start with the day that you left." She suggests, folding her arms across her chest.

I nod. *That would be the best place.* I think to myself.

"Sam, I did something that I hope you can forgive me for."

Her eyes close at my words. When she opens them, her hurt hits me full force. That sounded a lot better in my head. I take one step forward. She takes one step back. I take that as a sign to keep my distance.

"It's not what you think," I add.

"So, Valerie didn't answer your phone late at night on what was supposed to be a work trip?" Her fingers fly up to quote the last two words.

"It was a work trip, Sam. I invited her to come along."

Her eyes shoot daggers at me, and each one hits its mark. None of what I'm saying sounds remotely okay, but I continue.

"The day before I left, I saw Val having lunch with Garrett. I probably should have minded my own business and left it alone, but I couldn't. I couldn't stand by and watch him ruin her life. I had to do something."

Her expression softens, but only a little. She still looks as if she wants to murder me.

"We needed a designer for the new office. She has the experience, and I needed to get her away from him."

"And you didn't stop to think that maybe I should have known? You didn't think about how it would look to me, how it would make me feel?" Her voice cracks.

"You're right. I didn't think."

I take a step toward her. This time she doesn't move.

"I know it's no excuse, but we were barely speaking before I left. There was already so much between us that needed to be fixed. I was afraid that if I added Val to the mix, I'd lose you."

I take another step. Sam still doesn't move. She stands firm. I can see the war in her eyes. It's the same war I've had since I found out about her and Garrett. She doesn't know whether to trust me or let me go.

"And how do you explain the phone call?"

"Dad came to check things out and offered to take us out to dinner the night that you called. Val stopped by my room on her way down, but I wasn't ready yet. So, she waited. Nothing happened, baby. It was strictly business. All I wanted was to get back to you."

"You took your ex on a trip and kept it from me. You were alone with Valerie in your room Brad." Her voice cracks again.

She doesn't shed one tear. I can tell that she's trying hard to hold her emotions intact. She's hurting because of me.

I move toward her until we're mere inches apart.

"I don't want to lose you, Sam. I'm sorry that I didn't think. I'm sorry that I didn't tell you. I'm sorry about a lot of things, Sam." I place my finger under her chin and lift gently, guiding her eyes to mine. "But not as sorry as I would be if I didn't try to work things out with you. You're it for me, baby. No one and nothing is ever going to change that."

I dip my head to kiss her. She turns away and steps around me. I have to admit that it stings, her not wanting my touch as much as I crave hers. I knew that this would be hard for her. I didn't expect her to let me get as close as I did.

I turn around to face her only to be met by her back. Her arms are wrapped snug around her.

"Sam," I croak out.

She holds up one hand, stopping my next words. "I need some time, Brad. Can you give me that?"

I want to throw a tantrum and tell her no. I can't give her time. We need to finish this now. Then I remember where I am. I'm surrounded by a house full of people who care about her. They are here for her, no matter what. I don't want to be seen as just another guy who broke her heart. So, I relent.

"I'm going to leave Sam. Give you some time."

I wait for her to say something, anything, but she doesn't. My eyes roam the room until I find a pen and paper. I scribble a quick note along with the name of the hotel where I'll be staying and sit it on her nightstand.

Her silence makes the walk to her room door seem final. I pause with my hand on the doorknob. I don't bother looking back. Seeing her face will only make me want to stay and push harder.

"I love you, Sam," I say before walking out.

Chapter 8

Samantha

Seeing Brad brought forth a rush of mixed feelings. He said all of the right things, but I couldn't bring myself to forgive so easily. I know Brad. I know what he said is true, but it doesn't change the fact that he kept something huge from me. Two weeks and he never mentioned it. I sympathize with why he did it, but there was another way. There is always another way. He should've come to me. If he doesn't trust me with his judgment, then what will we become?

I nearly shattered when he left, but I couldn't be around him and think straight at the same time. I needed him gone so that I could process my thoughts.

Minutes later, I sit on the edge of the bed, pick up the note that he left, and read it.

"When you're ready, I'll be here. For as long as it takes. Aspen Hotel."

I run my fingers across the small piece of paper. Brad hasn't lost his touch with words. I look up when I hear a soft knock on my room door. I ignore it, hoping that they will go away. The knock sounds again.

"Grace. It's me. Lacy. Can I come in?"

I want to sulk, and cry, and wallow in my own self-pity. I want to force out tears that I've been holding back. I don't want to talk, but it may be just the thing that I need.

I sigh. "Come in."

Lacy peeks her head around the door. She comes in and closes it behind her when I nod. She walks over and sits next to me.

"I saw Bradley leaving. Is he coming back?" She asks.

"No. He rented a room at the Aspen."

"Oh. I see."

I turn to meet her concerned eyes. She wants to know why my eyes aren't smiling.

"Something is clearly on your mind. Would you like to talk about it?" She asks.

I contemplate spilling my guts and telling her everything. Every sordid detail.

"Can I ask you a personal question, Lacy?"

"Sure. Anything, Grace."

"What would you do if Robert kept something important from you because he feared it would break you two apart?"

Lacy gives me a strange look and straightens beside me. Her hand instinctively finds her belly.

"Well." She thinks. "I guess it would depend on the secret." She pauses again. "I would have to decide if the hurt he caused outweighed my love for him, or if it's something that I could move past and forgive."

I look away and ponder over her answer. What Brad did, it hurt, but it wasn't enough to make me cry. I could definitely move past it, but forgiveness is not an easy thing. He of all people should know that.

A gentle hand settles on my knee.

"Grace?" Lacy questions. "Do you still love him?"

My response is immediate and unfiltered. "I do. With all of my heart."

"Then go to him. Talk this out. Don't let it fester. It will only bring more doubt. Love may not always be enough, but sometimes it is. Sometimes it's strong enough to see you through the bad times, the mistakes, and betrayal. Sometimes it's enough."

I stare at her, wondering how I got so lucky. I let her words play through my mind.

Lacy continues. "I'm not telling you to forgive him." She pats my knee once. She glances into the bathroom and smiles. "He bought you Sunflowers for goodness sake. Have you ever known any guy who buys sunflowers? I'm guessing it has meaning." Her brows raise inquisitively.

I shrug and smile sheepishly. "It's sort of our thing," I say.

"That has to be worth something, right?"

"Do you know how much I love you, Lacy?" I ask, changing the subject. Lacy always gives the best advice, but I don't know if I'm ready to confront Brad again so soon.

Her eyes soften, and her smile grows wide with understanding.

"So, Grandma Liz and Grandpa Carl…" I wait for Lacy to respond.

"Yeah. What a surprise, huh?"

"The biggest," I say. "Have you talked to them yet?"

"Not really. Other than a hello, a hug, and a few smiles in passing, I've been pretty busy all evening. There hasn't been time. Not to mention, I don't know what to say to them."

I grab hold of Lacy's hand. "We can figure it out together."

The rest of the evening and into the night, we meet our dad's new love and get to know our mother's parents. Margaret is a sweet lady from what I've gathered, and I can tell that she makes dad happy.

Our grandparents filled in a few gaps for me about my mother, only things that they would know. They apologized for keeping their distance from us, even though they didn't need to.

I've always loved my grandparents, even though I didn't know them very well. I understood why they stayed away. I thought it was my fault, but they refuse to let me believe that. They didn't blame me for killing my mother as I'd thought. The reminder of her was just too great in us for them to bare until now.

I hardly slept last night thinking about what Lacy said. I wanted to go to him, but my pride wouldn't let me. He stayed true to his word and gave me my space. He didn't try to call me or text. I wonder if I made the wrong decision by letting things fester. I don't even know if he's still here.

When I arrive at the hotel, I realize that I don't have a room number, and chances are they won't give it to me if I ask.

"Excuse me," I say to the young girl behind the check-in desk.

She looks up to greet me. "Hi. Welcome to the Aspen. How may I assist you today?"

What do I say? What do I say? I think to myself.

I relax my right hand on top of the desk. "Hi...." I eye her name tag. "Hilary. My husband arrived yesterday ahead of me. He's not expecting me until tonight, but I was really hoping that I could surprise him." I say casually. "Would you mind telling me what room he's in?"

I smile and try to act natural. On the inside, my heart is pounding against my chest because of the lie I just told.

"We're not supposed to give out that information unless your name is on the reservation."

I continue to smile while feeling defeated inside.

"May I ask his name, please?" Hilary asks.

"Bradley Pierce." I wait for her to crush me even further by telling me he isn't here. I hadn't thought about how foolish I would appear if he is already gone. What kind of wife would I be if I didn't already know?

"And your name, ma'am?" Hilary offers a patient smile.

"Samantha Pierce." Brad's last name slides off of my tongue before I can think about it. Something about it feels right.

She punches a few keys on her keyboard, then looks up at me. "I see your name here, ma'am. Bradley and Samantha Pierce. I just need to see your ID."

I hesitate at first. My name isn't Samantha Pierce on my ID. Instead of panicking, I casually pull out my ID and hand it to her. She stares at it for a moment. Her face scrunches together in thought.

"Did you just get married?" She asks me.

"A few months ago," I fire off. "I haven't had a chance to do the whole name change thing." I laugh, and she joins in.

"Well, congratulations." She says. "You still have that newlywed glow."

I continue to smile, even while wondering if she needs her eyes checked. If she only knew the truth. I must be a better actress than I'd thought.

"Thank you," I reply.

She picks up a card, scans it through a machine, and hands it to me along with my license. "You're in room 315. The elevators are right past the waiting area to your left. Is there anything else that I can help you with?"

"No. That will be all. Thanks so much." I say before stepping away.

I'm still stunned when I reach Brad's room door. That went far better than I'd expected. Now I'm standing here trying to decide whether to knock or use the key that he obviously wanted me to have.

Five minutes go by with me standing here. I must look like a total nut job to the security team if they're watching. My mouth moves every couple of seconds as I talk myself through this. Of course, they don't know what I'm mumbling unless they're expert mouth readers. I place my head against the cold door a few times. I've turned and walked away over and over only to come back again. I go back and forth between holding the key to the slot in the door to raising my fist in the air to knock.

I blow out a deep breath and smooth out my clothing, deciding it would be best to knock. I raise my arm once again. Before my knuckles can meet the door, it swings open.

My breath hitches at the sight of Brad standing in front of me. A mix of feelings war their way through me. He's perfect, but he's not. I remember telling Lacy that something has to be wrong with him. He's too perfect. She told me, *"His flaws will surface soon enough."* Well, I guess I found one of his somethings.

My eyes skim the length of his chest to the black shorts that hang slightly off of his hips. It should be a crime to look like that. I force myself to think, even with the mountain of temptation blocking my way.

Brad clears his throat. My shameful eyes move away from dark territory and up to meet his.

"Sam. You came." His gruff voice sends a chill through me.

"I did."

"Do you want to come in?" Brad asks. "I knew you were here, but I didn't…" He pauses. "It should be your decision."

Great. I think. Not only am I on camera, but Brad witnessed my indecision too.

He steps aside to let me in. I walk past him and stop, leaving just enough room for him to close us inside.

Chapter 9

Bradley

She's here. I'll admit that I had my doubts when she didn't show up last night. I spent most of the night napping, waking up to check my phone just in case she'd left a message. There has to be a trail from the bed to the door from me trekking to look through the peephole into an empty hallway. Though, on my last check, I saw a glimmer of hope. She seemed nervous and indecisive, and I didn't want to influence her decision. So, I remained a peeping Tom, watching for some sign that she was ready to face me.

"I'm ready to hear you now." She says sadly.

"Would you like to sit?" I offer, nodding toward the sofa.

Sam sits on one end of the sofa. Her demeanor warns me to take the other end. I probably should take heed, but that would be too far away. So, I compromise and sit in the middle.

I've already told her what happened. There is only one thing that I want to make clear to her.

"It was a business trip, Sam. Nothing happened with Val. Nothing. I would never hurt you in that way." I wait for her to dispute my claim so that I can tell her again and again if necessary until she hears me.

Sam stares at me. It's not the *I want to murder you* stare from yesterday. I count that as a plus. Still, I'm expecting her to spout off at any moment with a rejection.

"Okay," she says.

"Okay?" I'm not sure I heard her right.

"Okay," she repeats. "I believe you, and I forgive you for keeping it from me. I even sympathize with why you did it." She pauses. "But Brad, something like that can never happen again."

"I understand that now," I say.

"You should have come to me first. We should have made a decision together." Her eyes fall to her lap.

I scoot closer to her until we're inches apart.

"I know Sam," I say to her.

I move closer. Our knees touch. Sam doesn't flinch or try to walk away.

"It will never happen again. I can't lose you."

I take one of her hands in mine. I cautiously lift her chin with my finger, hoping that she won't stop me again. My mouth salivates at the thought of kissing her. I need to taste her lips. I lean in halfway and stop. I search her eyes as she seeks mine. Her lips meet mine in a gentle kiss. Every cell within me comes alive with contact. I know immediately that this kiss is not enough. I want so much more. I want all of her. I fight against myself not to rush this, not to rush her. I push down my desire and pull away. I touch my forehead to hers. We're both breathing heavily from only a simple kiss.

"I love you, Sam."

"I love you too, Brad. You're still under my skin." She whispers.

"And you're under mine," I respond.

She tilts her head to meet my lips again. I pull her onto my lap, straddling my thighs. She deepens the kiss. Her tongue slides into my mouth, inviting me to tango. Her arms slink around my neck. Her fingers course through my hair. Her hips grind against me, causing me to swell beneath her.

I need to be sure that this is what she wants before we continue. I don't know if I can take much more of this without having all of her. I slow our kiss and pull away from her lips. Her head tilts as I leave a trail of kisses down her neck, ending with a lingering kiss to her shoulder.

"Sam." I plead her name.

She cups my jaw in her hands and stares into my eyes. "I need you, Brad. I want you." Her breathy tone sends a chill through me.

I respond by taking her lips all over again. I grab her by the ass and pull her as close as I can get her with the layers of clothing separating us. I manage to stand and carry her to the bedroom. She uncouples her legs and touches her feet to the floor. Her arms unwind from my neck. She takes a step back and strips down to nothing while never breaking eye contact. She spreads her legs shoulder length apart, silently telling me to come and get it.

She's still the most beautiful sight I've ever seen. Her body is a work of art made just for me. I trace two fingers from her collar bone through the stream of her chest and continue until I reach her warm wet center. I capture her lips in a slow, meaningful kiss. I dip two fingers inside of her, pumping in and out and in again, eliciting a moan from her.

"Mmm." Her low moan vibrates against my mouth, urging me to continue.

I extract my fingers and guide her to sit on the edge of the bed, deciding that she deserves more than a couple of lousy fingers. I spread her legs and drop to my knees between them. I smirk at her calculating stare. She wants this just as bad as I want to give it to her. I dip my head and lap at her sweet center. I wrap my arms around her thighs to hold her steady. I lick her long and hard, then nip at her tiny bud. Her thighs strain against my arms as her body trembles within my grasp.

I kiss her inner thigh and stand, but I'm not done with her yet. She deserves more after the way I've treated her these past weeks.

Her face is flushed, but there's not one ounce of regret about her. She pulls herself fully onto the bed until her head touches the pillow. I climb in, towering over her.

"That was..."

I Kiss the words out of her mouth and pull away. "Just the beginning," I finish.

She lifts her hips to meet my swollen length. I enter her slowly, savoring every inch until I fill her completely.

"Sam," I whisper her name. She feels so damn good.

"So good." She responds to my unspoken words.

She paws at my back, unleashing the gentle beast within me as I begin to move. She meets every thrust with ease. She returns every kiss with pleasure. She holds onto me as if she'll never let me go again, and I hold her even tighter.

"Brad. Yes." She says.

I love the way my name rolls off of her tongue. "I've got you, baby. Let go."

I pump hard into her when I feel her tighten around me. Her hands slap the bed at her sides, and she grips the sheet like a vise. Her back bows slightly as she ruptures around me. I continue to move in and out of her until my body stiffens, and my seed spills forth.

I roll over onto my back and pull her into my arm. I kiss her forehead, feeling grateful that she came back to me. I meant it when I told her that this was just the beginning. I wasn't only speaking of me making love to her. I was referring to the rest of our lives. I don't know what I would've done if I'd lost her.

Sam circles her finger on my chest. I've missed her so much.

"Brad."

"Huh?"

"Does this mean…" She pauses, halting her circular motion on my chest.

"You can ask me anything, baby," I say when she doesn't continue.

Her warm breath oozes across my skin before she speaks. "Does this mean that you forgive me too?"

I lift her chin to look at her. Her glossy eyes punch me in the gut. I've been so selfish in all of this. I neglected how much pain she must be in for my own selfish reasons.

"There was never anything to forgive. What happened to you was not your fault. I just needed time to deal with that. None of this is on you. Do you hear me?"

She nods as her tears seep out, coating my chest.

"If it makes you feel any better, though, I forgive you."

Her eyes snap to mine. I place a quick peck on her salty lips.

"I forgive you for thinking that I would ever let you go. Whether you want to hear it or not, you're stuck with me. My moods, my faults, my shortcomings, and long comings." I wiggle my brows playfully. "It's all yours. Even if you should decide that it's not what you want any more, I'm yours. Always."

We solidify the moment with a kiss, and with Sam nestled against my chest, with her leg flung over mine, we fall asleep together in the mid hours of the morning.

Chapter 10

Samantha

Brad and I fell into a rhythm when we returned home. For a while, I doubted that we would get back to this point, but it's better than it used to be. We were able to forgive, even though we haven't forgotten. We had a long talk, and Brad understands my reasons for not pressing charges on Garrett. We also agreed that he would get what's coming to him if everything goes as planned.

I had to return to work on Monday, and Brad has resumed his break since the setup project with his dad is done. Today, I have the day off. So, we planned to spend it together, but first, there's something that we have to do. I can't think of a better day than hump day to do it.

I replay the events of last night and this morning in my head while sipping my tea in the kitchen. Brad's oversized shirt hangs off of my right shoulder. I close my eyes and rub my cheek against it. I can still feel Brad's hands all over me. His kiss still lingers down my spine. The way that he...

"Am I interrupting something?"

Brad's voice startles me, causing me to jump and spill a small amount of my tea. He ignores it, wrapping his arms around me from behind. His lips touch the skin at the base of my neck, sending a jolt of pleasure through me.

"You shouldn't sneak up on me like that. If your arms weren't holding me in place, you would've felt the wrath of my tea." I say teasingly.

He chuckles behind me. "Oh, really."

I set my mug down and turn in his arms. "Yes, really." I hold his face in my hands and tiptoe to place a peck on his lips. "As much as I would love to romp with you all day, there are things to be done, Mister. We have a plan, remember?" I tap the sides of his cheeks playfully. "There's plenty of time for play later. I promise."

It's a promise I intend to keep. Brad and I have spent far too much time apart in the same space. There's a lot we have to make up for.

"I'm holding you to that," he says as he squeezes my backside.

"I know you will."

Brad's expression turns serious. "Are you sure that you want to do this?" He asks.

"I'm sure," I say without a doubt. "It's the worst that I can do and still keep my conscience clean."

He nods, then holds his lips to my forehead for a few seconds. He pulls back and looks at me. "If at any time you don't feel comfortable with her…"

I place my finger to his lips. "It'll be fine, Brad. I trust you. The hardest part about all of this is trying to convince her to play along. Do you think that she'll go for it? I barely know her."

"I know she will." Brad answers. "You may want to change out of my shirt before she gets here. Otherwise…" Brad leans in and teases my earlobe. "I won't be able to keep my hands off of you." He sucks softly on my bottom lip. "I don't think that's the kind of entertainment we're aiming for." He finishes.

"You are so bad," I say to him.

"And you are so good." He answers in the same way as always.

"Valerie. Please, come in." I answer the door when she arrives.

I'm more nervous about today than the first time that I met her. We're practically strangers. The only connection between us is Brad. I don't know how much Brad has told her about me, but I know her history. I know that she's not the least bit interested in love, and she is not a fan of bullies. I'll have to remember to keep that to myself considering best friends are supposed to guard each other's secrets, but Brad, being the man he is, wanted me to know. I guess he felt like me knowing would ease any fear I may have had about the two of them.

Valerie, on the other hand, doesn't seem nervous at all. She's still the picture of perfection. Every hair on her head is in place, and she greets me as if we've known each other forever.

"Hi, Samantha. Thanks for inviting me over."

During our talk, Brad told me that Valerie has no idea that I didn't know she was with him on their business trip. In her defense, she asked him, and he didn't give her a straight answer. As much as I wish to find some fault in her, I can't really be mad at her for that. Things weren't the best with Brad and me, and I give him credit for his part in all of this. In the end, it doesn't matter how I twist our story in my mind, the majority of the blame for all of it keeps coming back to me.

"Thanks for coming. Brad should be out in a minute."

Valerie takes a seat in the only single recliner in the living room and entwines her fingers together on her lap. I sit on the sofa close by.

Brad enters with a cool smile on his face and sits next to me. "Hey, Val. Glad you could make it."

I'll admit I'm a little uncomfortable sandwiched between Brad and Val. It's a bit of an exaggeration, but the room feels smaller than usual. They are coping far better than I am given their history.

Brad grabs my hand and gives it a simple squeeze. I relax, knowing that he's here for me.

"I'm sure you're wondering why we've invited you here." Brad addresses Valerie.

"I've had a few thoughts," she says.

"Before we get to the reason, Sam has something to share with you. Whatever you decide afterward, I'll accept it, one way or another. All I ask is that this conversation doesn't leave this room. There are only a few people who know about this. Treat her secret as you would one of mine."

Valerie nods, and Brad wraps his arm around my back, nestling me against his side. I fix my eyes on Valerie and begin by telling her who Garrett was to me. I proceed to tell her who he is now, what he's done to me, and how he betrayed someone that he called his brother. Valerie takes in every word. Her expressions range from happiness to sadness, to disgust, and ending in pity.

Pity.

It's a look that I've come to despise. It's the same one Brad gave me in the beginning before the truth of what happened really sunk in. I have to turn away from her to keep my emotions at bay.

We're all quiet for a few moments following my history. Brad unconsciously rubs his hand up and down my side. Valerie's otherwise prim demeanor falters. "That's..." She clears her throat. Her eyes wander between Brad and me. "... some story." Her eyes focus on me. "Did you consider going to the authorities?" She asks me.

I offer a sad smile. I can see why Valerie is Brad's best friend. They both have a way with words and are blunt to a point.

"I've considered that but decided against it. Regardless of what Garrett did, I don't want to ruin his life completely. I just want to teach him a lesson."

"Which is why we called you here." Brad chimes in.

Valerie gazes at us in confusion. "Where do I fit into all of this?"

"We want you to help us teach that lesson," Brad says. "If you're up for it."

"How am I supposed to do that?" she asks.

"Make him fall in love with you before you leave."

Valerie bursts into laughter until she realizes we didn't join in. "Wait, you're serious?"

"We are," Brad says.

"As I said before, I don't want to ruin his life. I just want him to feel what I felt when he tried to ruin mine." I explain.

"Do you think you can do it?" Brad asks.

"It shouldn't be too hard, right. We've been spending a lot of time together the past couple of days. He may be well on his way there already." Valerie smiles and averts her eyes to a point in front of her. She seems to be in deep thought.

"Val?" Brad questions.

"Mmhm?" She answers.

"If you don't want to…"

"I do. I will. I can do it." She fumbles her words. "I'll help in any way that I can."

It may seem petty to go this route to some, but I think it's for the best. I would rather Garrett live his life knowing what it feels like to truly love someone and lose them than to spend it behind bars stripped of his dreams and still not understand what real love is supposed to be. There is no lesson to be learned in the latter. He'll end up repeating the same mistakes, and the next time he may not be so lucky.

Chapter 11

Bradley

Now that Sam and I are back on track, I've had some time to focus on my job options. Linkin Engineering is still on my list, but I've been thinking a lot about what I want for us in the future. I'm not sure if that future is still here in Linkin. So, I'm meeting with David Rush today at Vanes Engineering in Munik, PA. Munik is where I've always imagined I'd end up eventually. It's also where my dad's new business is located. I've spent some time in the area growing up, so it's not completely foreign to me.

I was up before sunrise this morning so that I could beat the early traffic. The drive here was uneventful, but I was happy to make it. I have other business in the city once the meeting is over. They have a half days itinerary planned for me. Hopefully, it won't run over.

The receptionist perks up when she notices me walking toward her. Everything about her is too much for my liking, from the way she bats her lashes, to the sultry greeting she gives me. I can't see what she's wearing behind the tall desk, but I'm sure I'd feel the same about that too.

"Hello, welcome to Vanes Engineering. What can I do for you today?"

I make a point to keep my eyes focused on hers and not look in any other direction. I wouldn't want to give her false hope.

"I'm here to see David Rush."

"Do you have an appointment?"

"Yes," I say short and to the point.

"And your name, please." She seems annoyed by my disinterest and tones down her flirtatious behavior.

"Bradley Pierce," I answer.

She punches a few keys and picks up the phone next to her.

"Bradley Pierce is here for his meeting." She listens to what's being said through the receiver, then says, "Right away."

She hangs up the phone and steps around the desk.

"This way." She says to me.

I follow her around the corner to a row of elevators, where she stops in front of one of them. She presses the button to go up, and the elevator opens. I step inside, expecting her to follow, but she doesn't.

"Mr. Rush is on the twelfth floor. His assistant, Hannah, will meet you there."

I wonder if there is a reason why she had to walk me to the elevator to tell me that. I press button twelve. As the doors begin to close, she waves, and I hear her say through the small crack before we're cut off, "I'll be at the desk when you're done if you need anything."

The doors open to a lavish open area with a few seating options and a huge desk beside a set of double doors. I assume that the young lady sitting behind it is Hannah when she looks up at me and smiles. She stands to greet me with a firm handshake.

"Bradley Pierce, I presume."

I nod once. "Yes." I glance at her name tag. "Hannah."

"Right this way. Mr. Rush is expecting you."

I follow her into the office where David is sitting behind his desk. He stands and holds out his hand across the desk for me to shake.

"Bradley." He says cheerfully. "It's good to finally meet you in person." Then he addresses his assistant. "That will be all, Hannah. Thank you."

I hear the doors close behind me.

"Thanks for inviting me. I've been looking forward to it." I've wanted to come and see what they had to offer for a while now, but my uncertainty about other things held me back.

"Please, have a seat. We have a lot to discuss. I think you're going to like it here."

He speaks as if I've already accepted the position. I'll admit, from the outside looking in, it seems like it would be a great place to work if I'm going on looks alone. Other than the stalker receptionist on the main floor, I'm getting good vibes so far. I still have other things to consider before agreeing to take the job, with Sam sitting at the top of my list.

David spends the next three hours showing me around and introducing me to my colleagues, as he so eloquently put it. He took me to every floor and summarized what happens in different departments, giving me an understanding of the proper flow of the business.

I enjoyed every second of the tour, but when he showed me the view from what would become my office, I almost said yes on the spot. The office is located on the eleventh floor and is half the size of his, but ample enough to be comfortable in. The only furnishing inside is an L shaped desk and a four-tier bookcase. The windows are glass from ceiling to floor. David informed me that I would have a stipend for decorating to suit my style when I start.

In addition to everything else, they would allow me to rent one of the company-owned apartments if I needed it at a fraction of the cost.

After the tour, he took me out to lunch. I told him that I would need some time to think about it, but I'd get back with him soon. We part ways after lunch. I have mixed feelings. I can't decide if I did the right thing by prolonging my decision, or if I've just made a colossal mistake.

I spend the next hour looking at decorations. Then I stop by to check on my special project before I leave to go home. I'm anxious to tell Sam about my meeting. Though I can't imagine that she'll be too excited about the possibility of me having a job in another city.

Chapter 12

Samantha

My anxiety is growing by the day since Brad told me about his meeting at Vanes. I'm happy for Brad. I really am, but if he takes the job in Munik, where does that leave us? We'll never see each other. It's not an extremely long commute, but it will be once the long hours at work are factored into the equation. He will be working all day. I work mostly evenings. So, if by chance one of us does make the trip to visit the other, it will be in vain.

It annoys me that he hasn't thought about any of this. He keeps telling me not to worry. He hasn't taken the job yet, and if he does, everything will be fine. We will be fine. I can't fathom how he can be so confident. Sure, it may work in the beginning, but eventually, one of us will say enough is enough. One of us will give up and move on.

I thought that he'd given up on the idea of moving away, but he seems to have amped up speed this past week. He's had meetings every day this week. Today, he's out of town visiting another of his options. While I'm supportive of him exploring his possibilities, every time he leaves, I can't help but wonder if this time will be the last time. Will this opportunity be the one that decides our fate?

It's all I've been able to think about since he left an hour ago. I couldn't muster up the energy to get out of bed. So, I've been lying here looking at the blank screen on the television, watching my life play out before me, and imagining the many outcomes.

I jump at the sound of my phone ringing, drawing me away from my wayward thoughts. I sit up straight in bed when I see Emily's name on the screen. It's been almost two months since I've heard from my best friend.

I answer the phone, hurriedly. "Hi, Em!"

"Wazzup!" She drags out, causing me to laugh into the phone.

I've missed her so much. Besides Brad and Lacy, she's the only other person that I can confide in.

"I miss you. When are you coming home?" I ask.

"That's actually the reason I called. Cal had something come up, and we had to cut our trip short."

"So, when will I see you?" I know I sound like a lovesick mistress, but I don't care.

"How about now?" I hear some keys jingling through the receiver, and moments later, my doorbell rings. At first, I think it's a coincidence until it rings again.

"Em?" I question.

"Are you going to let me in or what?" She says.

I jump out of bed and speed walk to the door to open it. Joy washes over me at the sight of her standing there.

"Surprise!" She says, opening her arms to me.

I throw my arms around her neck. "Why didn't you tell me you were coming?" I ask.

"If I had told you, I would've missed this reaction."

We pull apart, and she steps inside and closes the door behind her.

"And you answering the door half-naked. If your neighbors weren't fully awake, I'm sure that did the trick."

My mouth forms an O. I tug at the hem of my tee in an effort to pull it past my thighs. I'd forgotten all about clothing the moment I knew it was her at my door.

"No need for that now. The doors closed. It's just us." She smirks. "You may want to check that sort of thing in the future before opening the door. Just saying."

I let go of my shirt, and we both burst into laughter until our eyes get misty. I can't remember the last time I had a laugh like this. I'm so glad that Em is here. There is so much that I want to tell her.

"You haven't changed one bit," I say.

She smirks. "How does that saying go? You can take the girl out of the city, but you can't take the city out of her mind."

"Uhm. I don't think that's how it goes, Em."

She waves my statement away. "You know what I mean."

I grab her hand and pull her over to the couch to sit. "You have to tell me everything. How was your trip? Did his family like you? Do you like them?" I fire off in rapid succession.

"I love his family, except uncle Billy." She scrunches up her face. "He was a piece of work. He low key tried to hit on me, and I still haven't decided if he was serious or just testing me to see if I'd go for it. I told Cal about it, you know, just in case uncle Billy tried to flip the story on me. He laughed it off like it was no big deal. Everyone else was cool, though. They didn't want me to leave." She leans in close like we're not the only two people in the room. "Between you and me, I had them eating out of the palm of my hands." She leans back. "There's not much else to tell unless you want to hear about Cal and me hooking up behind…"

"Okay, Em. I get it." I say, cutting her off. "Thanks, but no thanks." Both of us laugh.

"What about you? Any juicy details you'd like to spill?"

"Oh, I have something juicy. I'm not sure if you're going to like it, though."

Interest blossoms in her eyes. "That good, huh?"

I shrug. Em has no idea how good it was, and how bad it turned out to be.

"You may need a drink for this one," I tell her.

I grab us a stiff soda from the fridge. It's the strongest liquid that I could find at the moment. I relax back on the couch and begin to tell Em what happened, revealing just enough for her to get the idea. Em is stunned, to say the least. I've never seen her so quiet before.

When I'm done, she blows out a long breath of air and brushes her hand down her face.

"Why didn't you tell me she says? I could have... I don't know I could have done something." She looks just as broken as I was when I found out the truth.

I grabbed her hand and squeeze. "There is nothing that you could have done, Em. I didn't want to ruin your trip. And besides, what were you going to do? Come all the way back here? Leave your vacation and the man you love for me?"

"You should have called me at least. Let me talk you down from it. Talk you through it. I just feel so bad that I wasn't here. I knew Garrett was full of himself, but I never thought that he'd do something like that." She rambles on.

"It's okay. It really is. I'm okay. The hardest part about all of this is knowing what I put Brad through." My heart blanches at the thought. "The important thing is you're here now."

"I suppose you're right. There's a first time for everything." She says, attempting to lighten the mood. "You look like you could stand a day out. Do you have anything planned today?"

"If you count sleeping in and watching movies all day a plan, then yes. I do."

Em stands and pulls me with her. "While that sounds like loads of fun, I think we can do better than that," she says sarcastically. "That sounds like a plan for two, and I don't recall seeing Bradley anywhere. I swear you hit the jackpot twice, even if you went bankrupt the first time around," she croons. "Where is Bradley, by the way?"

I smile at her chatter. "He's exploring job opportunities," I say with a hint of annoyance.

Em gives me a confused look. "Is that a bad thing?"

"It wouldn't be if the offers were closer. I thought that we were in a good place, but now I'm starting to wonder."

Em grabs my hands and turns me to face her fully. "You are overthinking this. It's normal to want to explore every option before making lifelong decisions. Now go, get dressed, and let's have some fun." She guides me down the hall with her palms pressed against my back

    I go willingly, hoping that she's right about Brad.

Chapter 13

Bradley

I wish I could say that I was clueless about Sam's attitude in the last few days, but I'm not. I've noticed her hard looks and the uncertainty in her eyes. It's hard watching her frustration over my actions as she goes about her day. Though, there is one benefit to her vexed nature. I love helping her work it out in the bedroom. She's thrown me a few curveballs, blessing me with moves I didn't know she had.

I want her to know what I'm planning, but not yet. I'm committed to keeping this one last secret from her until the very last moment. I haven't told anyone, not even Gin. I still haven't made up my mind about the job, but whatever I decide, I want Sam by my side. Somewhere deep down, she has to believe that, regardless of how things seem on the outside.

I bend down to kiss her on her forehead, trying not to wake her. She worked late last night and couldn't wind down until well into the morning.

Her lips turn up at the corners. Her eyes peel open. "Are you leaving already?"

I sit next to her on the bed. "Sorry, baby. I didn't mean to wake you." I pay no attention to her morning breath and kiss her on her lips. "I couldn't leave without feeling some kind of skin," I say with a cocky grin.

"You are so full of it." She runs a hand down the side of my face. "Is this enough skin?" She asks.

I shake my head. "Not nearly enough."

"And this?" Her hand moves down my neck to my chest and slips under my shirt, resting over my heart.

I lean closer, kissing the base of her neck. She sucks in a sharp breath and lets it go. I pull back when the bulge in my pants becomes too much to bear. I wonder if I'll ever be able to touch her without wanting more. I hope it never gets to that point.

I kiss her once more. "One touch will never be enough," I say, rubbing my thumb across her flushed cheek.

"Are you sure about that?" She asks.

Her question alone makes me want to climb back into bed with her, but I won't. If I did, nothing that I have to do today would get done.

Dad called this morning and asked if I would stop by. By the sound of his voice, it's pretty severe. His request came across more like a demand rather than a question. It didn't seem right to try and worm my way out of it just so I could lounge around with Sam all day. He said it wouldn't take long. So, I should be back before it's time for Sam to go to work.

"Isn't it obvious?" I answer with a question. When I'm around her, I can't keep my hands to myself.

Her skin reddens further, signaling that it's time for me to go before things get heated. Even so, I ignore the warning, subjecting us to added torture. I bring her arm up to my lips and make a trail from the crook in her elbow to the sensitive spot on her wrist. Her eyes closed with contact.

"Mmm," she murmurs.

Her quiet delight is enough to drive me wild. I pull away from her to stand, trying to shake off the desire building inside of me.

"I need to go," I say.

Her pouty lips make me curse myself inwardly.

"I won't be long. When I get back, I'm gonna finish what I started."

She bites on a portion of her bottom lip, silently beckoning me to change my mind, to stay and finish now. I could oblige her, but I'd feel rushed. When I make love to her, I don't want to breeze through it. I need every motion and emotion to register.

I reluctantly back away from the bed. "When I get back," I repeat. "Keep it wet for me."

I keep my eyes focused on her long enough to witness the hitch in her breath. Then I turn and walk out of the room.

I hope this thing dad called me about is essential. I just walked out on a sure thing because of it.

"Mom! Dad!" I call out to them when I enter my childhood home. Instead of being met by my parents, Hale rounds the corner with a huge smile on her face.

"Hey, big brother. What brings you by today?"

I smile back at her and pull her in for a hug when she comes closer. I haven't seen much of Hale this year. She's just graduated from high school and is beginning to branch out. She's been spending most of her time away from home. I imagine that I'll see even less of her once she goes off to college. I don't even know if she's still planning to go.

"Hey, lil sis. What a nice surprise. It's been what? Six? Seven? Eight months?" I say jokingly.

"It hasn't been that long," she slaps my arm playfully. "Graduation was only a couple of months ago, silly." She looks around me. "Where is Samantha? I thought you two were joined at the hip."

"She's at home resting." *And waiting for me to satisfy her,* I think to myself. "She has work tonight. I actually came by to talk to dad. Is he around?"

Hale raises her brows. "Someone in trouble?" She asks.

I shrug. "I can't think of a reason why I would be. I am curious as to what's so important that couldn't wait."

"He's sitting on the patio out back. Don't leave without saying goodbye." Hale turns and walks toward the kitchen.

"I'll come to see you when I'm done," I say to her retreating form.

Dad is operating the grill when I step outside. He doesn't notice me right away. The sizzling noise must drown out my footsteps.

I find it odd that he's grilling. It's not even lunchtime yet. I let out a discrete snort to hold back a laugh that would probably earn me a scornful glare.

"Dad. What are you doing? It's nearly 9:00 am."

"Making brunch. Your mom and I couldn't decide on breakfast or lunch, so I thought I'd blend the two." He chuckles.

I look over his shoulders at the contents on the grill. My stomach rumbles with hunger.

"Any chance there's one for me?" I ask.

Dad laughs, but I'm serious. I had planned on grabbing something with Sam when I got back home, but a nice juicy steak with eggs is too good to pass up.

"There's plenty," he answers. "Why don't you go get mom and Haley. We'll eat first, then talk after."

I nod my acceptance and do as he says, even though I'm anxious to know what the big secret is.

I knock on mom's open bedroom door to get her attention. She turns away from the small mirror sitting on her armoire to see who it is. Her head is tilted into her bunched fingers, attempting to put her other earring in her ear.

"Bradley," she says. "Just in time." She gives me a quick hug. "Help me with this, will you?"

I help her with her earring. She seems to be on a mission.

"Dad asked me to come and get you for breakfast."

"Tell your father I'll be right there. I just received a call from my assistant. She's in crisis mode, so I have to leave earlier than I thought."

I leave mom to finish prepping while I deliver the message to Hale. Dad is already inside, whipping up some eggs when we walk into the kitchen. I help him set the table, and mom joins us a few minutes later.

After brunch, dad and I finally sit down alone in the living room for our talk. Dad is in the recliner next to me. He appears to be relaxed with his hands resting on the arms of the chair, but still serious. He looks like he's about to conduct a business meeting, sans the suit.

"I usually handle this sort of thing in the office, but I thought we'd be more relaxed here." He begins. "I've heard that you're thinking about taking a job in Munik." He waits for me to respond.

"I haven't made a decision yet, but it's a strong possibility."

"Does that mean you're also thinking of moving there?" He asks.

"If I were to take the job, then yes."

"Good." He says.

"Good?" I question.

"Since you're already thinking of moving, I wanted to run an offer by you. As you know, I need someone to manage the business in Munik."

I nod. "Yeah. You've mentioned it before."

"Well, I was hoping that you would consider taking the position," Dad says.

I swallow hard, hearing his words. "Wait. You want me to be the manager?" I can't believe what I'm hearing.

"Not only manage. I want you to run it the way you see fit. Of course, I'll be in the background, sort of like a silent partner that only gives an opinion when needed. But it's yours if you want it."

I was disappointed the first time dad told me he had someone in mind for the job. I had no idea that someone would be me. He's rendered me speechless.

Once his proposal sinks in, my first instinct is to say yes, but I can't make a decision like that without talking to Sam first. Can I? Out of all of the offers that I've received, this one is the most appealing. I would be my own boss, and I'd have dad by my side. There would be no one to answer to but me. I'll probably never get another chance like this.

"It's a very gracious offer," I say. "Can I have a few days to think about it?" I force my breathing to stay level while I'm bursting with excitement on the inside. I treat him like every other business owner that I've met with this past week. I show interest, but I don't want to appear too eager. So, I remain calm.

Dad sits up in the recliner. "Absolutely. Take some time. Talk it over with Samantha," he says pointedly. "Let me know when you've made a decision. For now, Chuck seems to be handling things well in my absence. Don't think too long. I'm not getting any younger," he adds with a chuckle.

"I won't." I'll have to have that talk with Sam much sooner than I thought.

Chapter 14

Samantha

I've spent the better part of my days hoping for the best and preparing for the worst. Brad has yet to discuss his future plans with me. I'm too much of a coward to bring it up. Is it wrong to pretend that everything will be fine? Is it foolish of me to have blind hope?

I've made up my mind that tonight is the night. We will sit down and have a conversation about us, and regardless of the outcome, I'll be okay with it. I have to be. I can't be mad at him for following through on his plans. It's what he's always wanted, long before he met me. Who am I to stand in his way?

I wonder if I would entertain the idea of moving away with him if he were to ask. I have ties here with work and school. It's not so easy to just uproot my life in hopes of a future with Brad.

I'm not sure about anything anymore. Brad supposedly had something very important to do today and encouraged me to call Em for some girl time. I can't wrap my mind around what could be so urgent on a Saturday to make him push me toward the company of someone else. Maybe he's distancing himself from me so that it will be easier on both of us when he leaves. The thought alone makes my stomach ache.

It's been him and me since the day that we met. Sure, we've had a huge hiccup in between, but it's always been him. When I look into my future, I see him and me, a mini-me, and a smaller version of him. I see a life filled with joy and pure pleasure. That's the life that I'm unsure about. It wouldn't work without him in it.

"Oh, no you don't." I hear Em shout next to me.

She dragged me out to a car show of all places. I don't know the first thing about cars, but she seemed to be excited about going. Her words were, *"Come on. It'll be fun. You'll see."* I haven't been able to appreciate any of the beautiful vehicles before me, because I can't stop thinking about my situation. I see, but nothing is registering.

"None of that today. No gazing off into space. No googly eyes that turn to sorrow. Only fun. And if there are tears, let them be tears of happiness. No sulking," Em says.

I've been spilling my guts to her since she has returned. She's taken it all in like a good friend, but she promised not to let me wallow in my thoughts. I love her for that. It's selfish of me, but I'm glad that her trip was cut short.

"I wasn't sulking," I lie. "I was merely thinking about what we should do next." I smile.

"You were so not," she says. "You've never been good at the lying thing. You should probably stop before your eyes bulge out of your head."

I give her a sidelong glance. She's never been good with idioms, but I keep that to myself.

"So, what should we do next," she asks, driving home her point.

"Hmm?"

"You were thinking, remember?" She laughs.

"I was, but you interrupted me before I could come up with something," I fire back.

The truth is, she's right. Thinking about it constantly only makes it worse. I push it to the back of my mind and try to enjoy the rest of the event.

After the car show, Em and I stop by One Stop Heroes for lunch. The place is jam-packed with people, but Em still insists on eating inside. Our other option would've been to go back to my apartment, and that would lead to me thinking about Brad again. Rather than fight her on it, I give in thinking it will be good.

We receive our order and sit at the only available table left inside. Em makes a comment about how good her sandwich is, and I try to give her my undivided attention, but I'm distracted by the golden locks on the other side of the deli. All I can see is the back of his head, but I know that it's Garrett. I would know that hair anywhere. My suspicion is confirmed when another customer steps aside to reveal Valerie sitting across from him.

We've only spoken once since she agreed to help us. She assured us that everything was progressing according to plan. From the looks of it, they're still going strong. Garrett holds out his hand on the table, and she fills it with her own. He must say something funny because she begins to laugh. From the outside looking in, one would think that they are madly in love. I must say that I didn't believe that she would be able to pull it off, but she appears to be an outstanding actress.

I'm content watching their interaction. Not because Garrett and Val appear happy, but just knowing that what Garrett thinks is real is all a ruse. By this time next week, he will have lost someone that he cares deeply about. I keep telling myself that this was the right thing to do, that he'll learn something valuable from this experience. I'd convinced myself that this was not just to satisfy some sick need to punish him, that this wasn't just for my benefit but his as well. But watching him pawn over her is giving me more joy than I imagined.

"Are you even listening to me?" Em breaks my concentration.

"Yeah, I am."

She looks back in the direction I was just staring in. "Mmhm. Sure, you are. Who is that anyway? Is that?" She squints her eyes in that direction. "Is that Garrett?"

"It is. I can't seem to get a break from the guy," I say.

"I should go over there and give him…" Em stands mid-sentence. I grab her hand, pulling her back to a sitting position.

"No, Em. Please don't."

Em knows all about our plans with Valerie. They've never met, but she declares she likes her already. Garrett, on the other hand, she wants to hurt badly.

"I don't want an audience. He hasn't seen us. Maybe that's a good thing," I mutter.

She sighs heavily. "Only because you asked nicely," she says. She shoves her thumb over her shoulder. "Is that Bradley's ex?" She asks.

I nod, knowing this will open up a whole new line of questioning. I brace myself for the onslaught.

"Wow! She's pretty." She pauses.

Tell me about it. I think to myself. It's nothing that I haven't noticed before.

"Not as gorgeous as you, of course," Em adds. She glances back again. "They look cozy."

"Yeah. They do, don't they?" I smile at the two of them.

"If I had known that this was what it took to make you happy, we could have stalked them earlier."

"That's ridiculous, Em. I would never..."

"Go on. Admit it. You're enjoying this." Em cuts me off.

I shrug. "Maybe just a little." I glance in that direction and catch Val's eyes. Her smile doesn't falter. She gives me a discreet nod and returns her attention to Garrett. He doesn't seem to notice the contact between us.

I turn my attention away from them as we eat. Though I'll enjoy the outcome of all of this, I don't want to watch Garrett's every move with another girl. That would make me crazy.

When she's done eating, Em says, "I need to empty the bladder. I'll be right back."

She doesn't bother asking if I want to come with her, because that would mean I'd have to walk past the happy couple. Valerie stands and walks in the same direction as Em. I pull out my phone to distract me while she's gone.

"May I?" A familiar voice drawls out, requesting my attention.

I look up from my phone. After all this time and everything that's happened, I still think Garrett is a handsome guy. If only he were as attractive on the inside.

"Now is not the time Garrett," I whisper shout.

"I'll be quick. I promise."

I wonder if he'll go away if I refuse. *No. It's not his style.* I answer silently. He'll likely make a scene to draw attention to us.

"Fine, but make it fast." I relent.

He sits across from me. His hands disappear underneath the table. I watch him, waiting to hear what lie he'll tell next.

"I'm sorry, Samantha." His expression looks sincere, but I don't want to believe him.

"What?" I ask.

"I said, I'm sorry. I know that I've hurt you more than you deserve. All I've ever wanted was you." He pauses. "I couldn't stand the thought of you with someone else. I fucked up. I know my words don't mean much, but I am sorry. I want you to be happy, Samantha. If that means you being with someone else, then I can live with that. I would never admit it to him, but Brad is a better man than I'll ever be." He chuckles. "You deserve a better man."

My mouth opens and closes in dismay.

"I know you're not ready, but one day I hope you can forgive me." He stands and walks away, leaving me wide-eyed and open-mouthed. He returns to his seat across the deli like nothing ever happened.

I'm staring at the back of his head when Em returns. She waves her hands in front of my face.

"Samantha. Are you alright? Did something happen?"

"More like someone," I answer.

"What did he do now?" She asks.

I look at her. "He apologized."

She wrinkles her forehead. "From across the room? You told me he was good, but I didn't think he was that good."

"No. He was here. Sitting in the same seat that you're in. He blessed my relationship with Brad, as if I needed it, and asked for my forgiveness." I let out a breath of frustration. "That's the thing with him. He's a sneaky bastard, and he's unpredictable. I never know what to believe. But somehow, this time feels different. I believed every word he said. I believe that he truly feels regret."

"This probably won't make you feel better, but that girl, Valerie, sent a message. She wants you to know that he's not the same guy that she first met. He's changing."

Em is right the majority of the time. Valerie's message made me feel worse. I'm torn. A lesson needs to be learned, but I don't want to hurt him. I want him to be happy too. There's nothing that I can do now to stop what's already happening.

Chapter 15

Bradley

I've never really understood the meaning behind the saying, "make an honest woman out of her." Everyone always has an opinion about what's right and what's wrong, but they don't notice their own wrongs and misgivings. I've seen marriages happen and crumble just as fast.

I promised myself three things when it comes to Sam and me. One, I wouldn't be the guy who listened to what everyone else thought was right. Two, I wouldn't base my relationship on the likes of others. Three, when the time was right, when we are both ready, I would know it without a doubt. That time for Sam and me is now.

I want to make her an honest woman, whatever that means. I didn't make the decision because I was pressured into it, or because it's the right thing to do. I made the decision because I love her, and the timing couldn't be more perfect than now. And thinking selfishly, my last name would look good on her. Everything is falling into place, and she is a part of my everything.

I'm not the least bit nervous when I walk into Reynaldo's. They aren't open yet, but they agreed to meet with me. Sam mentioned to me before how much Vivian likes me. So, I'd hoped that it would work well in my favor when I reached out to them. She spoke with the manager, and he said I could come right over.

So here I am, about to take one of the most significant steps of my life.

Vivian guides me to the office in the back where Jeff sits, waiting for us behind his desk. I didn't tell her why I wanted to meet, just that it's about Sam and it's important. But I think she knows exactly why I'm here, judging by the broad smile on her face.

I walk inside and shake Jeff's hand before sitting across from him. Vivian takes the seat next to me.

"We finally meet face to face," Jeff says. "Samantha has nothing but good things to say about you. She's a sweet young lady and one of my best employees. Any friend of hers is a friend of mine."

"Thank you, Mr. Reynaldo," I respond.

"No thanks necessary. Everyone around here calls me Jeff. How can we help?" He shoots straight to the point.

"He's planning a proposal," Viv says to Jeff before I can speak. "Aren't you," she turns to me and waits for a response.

I hold back my laugh.

"Viv," Jeff says amusedly. "Let the poor guy speak."

"What? Am I lying?" She looks between the two of us. "There are only two reasons a man would behave like this. She's either pregnant, or he wants to marry her. Which is it?" She asks me.

Jeff and I are both entertained by her. Sam was right. Vivian is spunky. I like her.

"I want to marry her," I answer.

Vivian gives Jeff an *I told you so* look and crosses her arms over her chest.

"So, what do you need from us?" Jeff asks.

"I was hoping that you had a last-minute cancellation for tomorrow night." I've been told that this place is booked up for months at a time. It's hard to get a last-minute reservation because they rarely have cancellations.

Jeff and Vivian share a smile. I swear they're talking to each other through their minds. I hope that it's a good sign for my sake.

"We don't have any cancellations," Jeff begins, and my heart falls. "But we do have a private room available."

"A private room?" I ask in disbelief. "That would be perfect. How much?"

"I'll let you book it for…" Jeff lets out a grunt when Vivian kicks him under the desk. He gives her a hard look. "I'll tell you what… If she says yes, it's no charge. If she says no, you owe me half price for wasting our time."

I say, "Deal," even though his proposition shook me. It wasn't the money that drew my attention. If his price were in the hundreds or even one thousand dollars, I'd pay it. What got my attention was hearing that there's a chance that she might say no. I'm selfish, and I think that we're ready for the next step. What if she doesn't feel the same?

After we go over the details for tomorrow night, I thank them again before I leave. I stop by the jewelry store to pick up Sam's ring. I pulled it out of my secret hiding spot earlier in the week and dropped it off to have it engraved.

The more I think about the first time I was going to propose, the more I know it wasn't the right time. Everything that happened was for a purpose, leading us to this day, and this place in time. I plan to make tomorrow one of the best days of her life.

Chapter 16

Samantha

Somewhere between seeing Garrett and Brad returning home yesterday, I lost my nerve to question Brad about his plans.

Lately, nothing good has come from my encounters with Garrett, including yesterday. He apologized, and I believe him, but his confession makes me question everything. If someone with a heart as dark as Garrett can do a complete one-eighty, then someone with a heart of gold can do the same. The arrow goes both ways. With Brad's stranger than normal behavior, I don't know which way his arrow is leaning.

I didn't bother getting out of bed this morning. Viv left a message this morning, giving me the day off, explaining something about last-minute cancellations. She said she could handle it unless I wanted to run the show by myself. She said there's no use in both of us being there for such a small crowd.

Reynaldo's has never had a small crowd, but I don't question her. I take it as a sign from the universe that I need a day to rest.

Brad was up early this morning again, but I don't think that he left the apartment. I pretended I was asleep when he snuck out of our bedroom. I've tried to pinpoint it, but I can't seem to figure out his need to stay away from me during our wakeful hours when he holds me so tenderly during the night.

My eyes remain closed when I feel him enter the room. I keep my breathing even and try not to move. I'm curious to see what he does next.

I hear something tap against the nightstand. To my surprise, the bed sinks a fraction next to my thighs. A shadow falls over me. Then I feel warm lips against my cheek.

I smile and peel my eyes open as if I were just waking up. "Good morning," I utter when my eyes find Brad's.

"Morning beautiful. I hope you're hungry," he says, nodding to the nightstand.

I peer up over my lashes and breathe in the delicious aroma. "What is it?"

"My specialty. Toast. Eggs. Bacon. I even threw in some fruit," he says, feeling proud of himself.

I pull myself up into a sitting position on the bed. "Is this a special occasion?"

"Does it have to be?" He asks slyly.

"No, but…"

"No buts. I just wanted to do something nice for you. As a matter of fact, I wanted to take you out today before work. I've been so preoccupied lately. You should let me make it up to you."

I raise my brows. "I should?"

"I think you should. I'm usually right about these things." He tucks my hair behind my ear.

"Okay, but one small change in detail," I say.

"What's that?"

"You're stuck with me all day. Viv gave me the day off."

He appears to be in deep thought for a moment.

"In that case, I know just the thing to complete our evening."

"What did you have in mind?" I ask.

"Since you have the whole day, we have time for a little R, R, & S," he says, wiggling his brows.

"S?" I question.

"You know, a little bit of this." He touches his thumb to his chest. "And a little bit of that." He nods his head toward me.

I slap his arm playfully. "You're such a goof."

There's something different about him this morning. He has a twinkle in his eyes. He's relaxed. He's happy. He's acting weird but in a good way.

Brad and I spent the morning doing everything that he suggested; a little R&R and a lot of this and that. We've been more in contact in one morning than we have the entire week. I still think he's acting weird, but I don't mention it. I'm enjoying this time with him.

"You're really not going to tell me where we're going?" I ask him once we're in the car.

"It's a surprise, but I'll give you a clue." He pauses, then smirks as he continues with the clue. "I'm dark, but can be light. I'm empty but easily filled. I can be cold or warm. I wake up just before the sun peaks and go to sleep after midnight."

I watch his profile from the side, trying to think of what it could be, but nothing rushes forward. "What kind of a clue is that?" I giggle.

He chuckles. "It's one that you'll never guess," he replies smartly.

A few minutes later, we pull up to Watcher's Theatre. It's been months since we were last here. I still remember the first time like it was yesterday. So much has happened since then. Our experience has aged us in such a short amount of time.

Brad parks the car and takes the keys out of the ignition, then turns slightly in his seat to face me. He grabs hold of my hand. His expression turns serious.

"Do you remember our first time here?" He asks.

"I do. I was just thinking about how much we've grown since then."

"I remember everything about that night, Sam. How hesitant you were at first. The way you lay your head on my shoulder and snuggled into me. I didn't know how it would happen, but I knew that you would be the center of my life. That was the start of us, where we began to love each other."

"I remember," I say, smiling. "You were so confident in your pursuit. You made me feel like every decision was my own when there was never a choice to be made. I remember feeling disappointed that you knew what the movie was about because that would mean that I wasn't the center of your attention. How crazy is that?" I giggle.

"Not crazy at all," he answers. "Everything about you scared me, but my fear was nothing compared to my desire to be with you. That need is still just as strong as the first time I heard your voice." He rubs his thumb across my cheek. "I don't ever want to forget Sam. I want to remember the wheres and hows and whys forever because, without them, we wouldn't be."

I stare at him in awe. Brad can be playful, assured, even a little boastful at times. But there's this other side to him that cuts straight to my heart. His words. His eyes. His touch. His heart is so full and so powerful. I'll never understand what I did to deserve someone like him.

His eyes bleed into mine. "What did I do to deserve you?" He whispers.

Our lips meet across the armrest. Slow. Tender. Kind. All of my senses jump to life. We're both caught up in the moment, our hands moving over one another. I try to pull away when I hear distant giggles outside the car. Brad draws me back for one more kiss. My lips tremble when he pulls away.

He watches me as I touch my fingers to my mouth. I want more of this and that. Right now.

"Me too," he smirks, reading my mind. He retreats to his side of the car and rests his head on the driver's seat. "Ready to go inside?"

"I thought you'd never ask." I can't stay in this car one minute longer without jumping his bones. I don't wait for him to come around and open my door. I jump out before he does or says something else to make me stay.

Chapter 17

Bradley

This time, just like the last, I let Sam choose the movie. She didn't pick a sob story as I'd hoped she would. She chose something humorous rather than something to snuggle up to. I suppose I shouldn't have laid it on so thick before going inside.

I gave in after the movie was over and told her I was taking her out to dinner, but I didn't mention where. The look on her face when we pull up at Reynaldo's is priceless. It's a mix of confusion and surprise. I couldn't have planned it better.

"Uhm, is there a reason that you brought me to work?" Sam asks, puzzled.

"For dinner," I respond. "I figured since Vivian said that it's a slow night, we shouldn't have a problem getting a table. Unless you're not hungry." I shrug. "We could grab takeout and go home."

"No. I want to go inside. Though, I wish I would have known. I would've dressed for the occasion."

The only opinion that matters is mine, and I think she looks perfectly fine in her black jeans and t-shirt. We'll be separated from the crowd anyway.

"You are dressed for the occasion. Who cares what anyone else thinks? You're beautiful, Sam. Trust me. They won't even notice." I wink, earning a blush from her.

We stop at the concierge desk once we're inside. Sam looks around the restaurant, her eyes exploring the full space. Every table is occupied. I notice her look of hesitation turn to one of disappointment.

"Hey, Samantha!" The girl behind the podium greets her.

"Hey, Carla," Sam says. "What happened? Viv told me there were a bunch of cancellations, but from the looks of things..." Her voice trails off.

"Cancellations? It's business as usual." Obviously, Carla has no idea what Sam is talking about.

I take that as my cue to speak up. "Hi, Carla. Reservation for Pierce."

Sam cranes her neck to look at me. I give her my signature smirk.

Carla finally seems to notice me. "So, you're the infamous Brad?" She questions.

She and Sam share a look. Sam doesn't dare look at me, but I detect a soft shade of red tinting her skin. I wonder what Sam has revealed about me to her co-workers.

Carla clears her throat and re-composes herself. "It's nice to finally meet you." She glances down at the log in front of her. "You're our last arrival for tonight. The room is ready for you."

"Brad?" Sam inquires. "What's going on?"

"It's just dinner, baby. Relax. Live in the moment with me." I slip my arm around her waist and kiss her temple.

"You wouldn't happen to have another one of him lying around, would you?" Carla jokes, stealing our attention back.

Sam shakes her head, seemingly still in shock. "Nope. Only one."

"Well, darn." Carla sighs heavily. Then she motions for a young man to come over. "If you'll follow Marty, he'll take you back."

We follow Marty back to an elegantly decorated enclosed room. A single chandelier glistens from the ceiling. Sam and I sit at the only table inside. It's cozy, but there's enough space around us for a dance if we wanted to.

Marty gives us two menus and steps to the far side of the room. He looks like he wants to say something to Sam, but he's trying his best to be professional. Marty pours us a drink, and when we're ready, he takes our order and leaves the room.

We sit in silence for a couple of minutes, staring into each other's eyes. I wait for Sam to speak first. I want to know what she's thinking. This has to be a lot to take in, being here in the one place where so many women's hope becomes a reality. Us being here indicates that I'm ready to take the next step in our relationship. I wasn't nervous about asking her until now. I usually have an idea of what's in that head of hers, but tonight is different. Her expression is indescribable.

"When did you plan all of this?" She finally speaks.

"Yesterday, while you were with Emily. I'll have to thank Jeff and Vivian again for helping me out."

"So, you're the reason why she lied to me." Sam grins.

I hold my hands up in surrender. "Guilty as charged. I couldn't think of a better way to keep the surprise hidden."

"I'll excuse all of you, just this once because I haven't eaten since this morning. And I'd like to actually enjoy the place for once."

"I want to be completely open with you, Sam, about what I want and where I want to be."

Her body stiffens as she takes in my statement. "Okay." She takes a sip of her drink.

"Before I met you, I imagined this whole other life for myself that's a stark difference from the one I'm living. But that's not a bad thing. With you, I've learned to love the right way. I've grown into a man that I'm proud of. My stance on life and my career has changed. This past week, I've met with a lot of companies in search of something permanent. I would probably still be searching if I hadn't been presented with the perfect opportunity."

"I had a talk with my dad on Friday." I continue. "He wants me to run the new office in Munik."

She watches me closely, swallowing deeply.

"I want to accept his offer, Sam." I pause to let my words sink in. "I used to think that my place was here in Lakin, at least for the foreseeable future. But that's not true anymore. I feel that it's time to move on and start fresh."

Her eyes gloss over. She sits straighter in her chair.

"But I don't want to move on Sam if you're not with me."

She sucks in a breath of air and lets it out slowly. I see her visibly relax.

"I want you to come with me. I know that you have a life here, a job, school, and leaving is not as simple as it sounds, but I'd like for you to consider it. If it's not what you want. If you want to remain here, I'll understand. I still want to take the job. I'll just have a longer commute if you decide to stay because there's no way that I'm giving up on us."

"It will never work," she says. "I could never ask you to drive hundreds of miles every day just to make it home to me. That would be selfish and unrealistic."

I try to wrap my head around what she's saying. Is she giving up and letting me go?

She leans forward, resting her arms on the table. "You should take the job. It's a sensible move. Whether I go or not shouldn't matter, but if it eases your mind, I want to go with you. There will always be another job and another school, but there can only be one you."

"Are you sure about this? You have to know that I would never force you to give up what's important to you for my sake."

"You're not forcing me. You asked, and I've decided. I choose you, Brad, every time."

"What are you going to do about school and work?"

"I'll think of something. We'll figure it out together."

As much as I want her with me, I don't want her to resent me for taking her away from everything and everyone that she's grown to love.

Chapter 18

Samantha

Over dinner, I have time to think about my choice to fly blindly with Brad. He posed a valid question. What am I going to do? It was one of those instances where my mouth spoke before I truly had a chance to process what I was saying. The only thing that mattered at the time was us. I meant every word, but now I need a plan. I would have to transfer to a different school and find a new job. He didn't mention where we'd be staying.

"Have you started house hunting yet?" I ask after finishing up my food.

He smiles. "I have something in mind, but it's a surprise."

"You and your surprises. And don't even bother giving me a clue. The last one didn't help at all," I say as we both laugh.

Brad stands and walks over to my side of the table.

"Would you like a celebratory dance?" Brad asks.

I take his hand, and he ushers me out of my seat, pulling me close to him. His hands rest on the base of my back. There's a remote to control the music, but we ignore it. I rest my head on his chest as we began to dance slowly to the melody in our heads. For the first time in a couple of days, that old familiar feeling of security returns to me. We stay wrapped in each other's arms for what seems like hours.

"Sam."

There's something in the way Brad says my name. Before I can decipher it, a low vibrating ring sounds from my purse. We glance in the direction where the noise came from. I ignore it, not wanting anything to ruin this moment. I feel like this is it, the moment when he pops the question.

"Sam." He says my name once more, this time staring into my eyes.

And again, the phone chimes in, interrupting him.

"You should probably get that," he says. "Whoever it is, they're pretty insistent. It could be important."

"Are you sure? They could wait until after…" I stop mid-sentence, not wanting to make a fool out of myself. What was I going to say? They could wait until after you propose. And suppose that's not our reason for being here. I would be beyond embarrassed. "Hold that thought," I say instead.

Before I can get to the phone, it stops ringing, but quickly goes off again. The name Dad alights the screen. Fear grips my chest. It has to be Lacy if dad is calling.

I answer hesitantly. "Hello. Dad, is everything okay?"

"Hey, Sammy," dad says much livelier than I'd expected. "I'm sorry if I'm interrupting, but you were adamant about receiving updates about Lacy."

Brad is now standing by my side with a concerned look on his face. I whisper to him, *"It's my dad."* He nods and remains by my side.

"It's fine, dad. Is Lacy alright? Is it the baby?" I ask anxiously.

"The baby is fine. Lacy, on the other hand, is fighting labor pains."

My mouth forms an O. "She's in labor?" I ask. "Right now?" I can hardly believe it. "But it's not time yet," I protest frantically.

"That shouldn't be a problem. Her due date is in two weeks. So, she's past the point of concern," dad replies.

I look at Brad, silently letting him know that I want to be there. He tries to console me by rubbing circles on my back.

Brad whispers in my open ear, "Let him know we're on the way. I'll go settle the bill." He kisses my temple and leaves me to go and speak with Marty.

I stop thinking in those few seconds to appreciate the man that I'm going to spend the rest of my life with. With one look, he read my emotions and answered my unspoken plea.

"We're leaving now. Tell Lacy to hold baby Thomas inside until I get there."

Dad laughs at my absurd comment. Though not reasonable, I'm totally serious. I don't want to miss the birth of my first niece or nephew, and I would never forgive myself if something happened to Lacy, and I wasn't there to say goodbye.

We stopped by the apartment to grab a few things before we left. A few hours after dad's call, we arrive at the hospital. I figured Lacy would be either too busy or too tired to be bothered. So, I kept in contact with dad through a series of text messages on the ride here. Baby Thomas is literally still hanging in there.

Once inside, I'm shown to Lacy's delivery room, per her request. Brad remains in the lobby with my dad.

Lacy smiles through her breathing when I walk into her room. "Grace," she manages to say in between. "I'm so glad you're here." She reaches for me to come to her bedside. "No offense, honey." She says to Robert.

"None taken." He brushes her sweat laced hair away from her forehead. "I'm going to step out for a few minutes and update the guys."

If I didn't know any better, I'd think that he's happy that I'm here too and welcomed the break. I give Lacy my full attention when Robert leaves the room.

I pull a chair up to the bed and take her hand again. "You've been at this for hours. How are you feeling? What can I do to help?" I ask, knowing that there is not a whole lot that I can do. I can't give her what she really wants, and that's to have this baby out of her.

"Don't worry about me. I'm fine," Lacy lies. "Or at least I will be once the little one decides to make a debut."

"Hey, little one. Take it easy on your mama," I say to baby Thomas, who immediately reacts to my voice. A tiny foot, or maybe a knee pokes at Lacy's belly.

"I think he knows your voice," Lacy says.

"He?" I question.

"No. We still don't know yet, but nice try." She laughs, then lets out a low scream. When her breathing evens out, she says, "I guess you were the holdup. Will you get Robert?" She breathes out. "And the doctor?"

I rush to the waiting room to retrieve Robert. Everything happens quickly after that. The doctor comes in accompanied by two nurses. Lacy's feet are propped in the stirrups. I hold one hand, while Robert holds the other. Fifteen minutes later, baby Thomas is born. He's tiny but breathing fine on his own. He has a head full of hair and screams at the top of his lungs. I'm not at all surprised by how fiery he is. I half expected it, given the way he reacted to my voice when he was still inside.

What I am surprised by is the second baby that makes an entrance six minutes later. She's a little smaller than her brother and needs help breathing at first, but the doctor is hopeful that she'll be fine. I've been calling her Cloak. I think it fits, given the fact that she's been hiding from all of us this entire time.

Lacy made it through labor without any complications. Her biggest heart rate spike was learning of Cloak's existence. Now she's anxious about the second set of inventory that she instantly needs. None of that seems to faze Robert as he stares down at their two bundles. Once the shock wore off, a permanent smile formed that hasn't worn off yet.

Chapter 19

Bradley

We've been waiting for almost an hour to hear news about the delivery. Sam came in a hurry to get Robert, and we haven't seen either of them since. It's awkward, to say the least, sitting out here with Sam's dad, but not because I'm afraid to be alone with him. He keeps glancing at me as if he knows about our almost engagement. I wonder if this is a good time to tell him about our plans. He may not be too keen on the idea of his baby girl moving even further away from him. Though he does seem to have his hands tied with the lady by his side. This may be a perfect time, except I can't seem to form the words. And besides that, I don't want to take attention away from Lacy. Through everything, the prospect of this baby is the one thing that's kept Sam preoccupied.

I turn my head, focusing my eyes on the hallway beside the receptionist's desk. I feel Sam coming before I see her turn the corner. She's breathing like she just ran a marathon, and she's smiling from cheek to cheek. Everything must have gone well. Donald and I both stand at the same time upon spotting her. Sam stops between us, waving her hands through the air excitedly.

"It's a boy!" she shouts, trying to keep the tone of her voice as level as possible and failing.

"I knew it would be a boy," Donald says proudly.

Sam bounces on her toes like there's more to tell. I've never seen her this excited about anything before.

Her eyes flicker between the two of us. "It's a boy," she says again. "And a girl," she adds.

Donald's eyes bulge, hearing Sam's words. "What?" he asks.

"We have twins, dad. Twins. Can you believe it?"

Donald stumbles back into the chair. "Twins," he says in disbelief.

I smile, but don't voice my opinion on the matter. This is their moment. I'm just along for the ride.

"Twins," she repeats as if she still can't believe it. "Robert Brody Jr and Amber Renee, who's already earned a nickname."

A small sniffle comes from Donald when he looks at Sam. "Amber?"

Sam offers him a knowing smile. "Yes. Our little Cloak," Sam answers. "Mom and babies are doing fine. Cloak has to stay in the NICU for a few days for observation, but she's perfect, dad. They both are.

"When can we see them?" Donald asks anxiously, overlooking the fact that Sam nicknamed his grandbaby Cloak.

"Shouldn't be long. Robert said he'd come out and get us once they were cleaned up and settled into the room."

I love seeing her this excited about kids. I look forward to the day when we have one or two or three of our own. If she wants a team, I would happily supply the sperm. I know that she'll be the best mom, even though the idea frightens her. Maybe seeing her sister through this will help ease some of her fear about having children. Lacy is proof that childbirth doesn't have to end in tragedy. What happened with her mom is not the way it has to be.

Her gaze is full of hope when our eyes lock in a private dance. It warms me from the inside out. I want to give her everything her heart desires and share with her all of mine.

Donald blows out a deep calming breath, slicing through our connection. It pains me to look away.

"Two babies." He says again while shaking his head from side to side.

All of this talk about babies makes me want to bury myself in Sam. I need some fresh air. My eyes return to Sam. "I'm gonna step outside. You look like you could use a break. Want to come along?" I ask her.

"Sure." She bends to kiss her dad on his cheek, and we walk out together.

Once we're outside, we secure a spot on one of the hospital benches. Sam props one leg up on the bench facing me. Her smile doesn't waver.

I watch her with sheer fascination. I don't remember ever discussing having children with her.

"Do you want kids, Sam?"

Her smile lessens, but it does not fade. Judging by her reaction, all signs point in the direction of maybe or not. I want children, but I want her more. So, if her answer is no, then I can live with that.

"Do you have baby fever?" she asks.

I shrug. "I was just wondering. It's not something that we've discussed, and I know how hard it's been for you." I try to act nonchalant. I don't want her to feel like it's a must that she says yes because that's far from the truth.

Sam tilts her head to the side in thought. I wait patiently for her to form her next words.

"I've been afraid of having kids for a very long time." She pauses and takes my hand in hers. "But Lacy's experience has cracked my mind wide open. Seeing not only one, but two strong babies and a healthy Lacy makes me want that for myself. For us. If that's something you want," she adds.

"Honestly, I hadn't given it serious thought until tonight. If it were only you and me for the rest of our lives, I would be perfectly fine with that. Children would be a bonus, but not a requirement." I hold her stare, making it clear to her that she is enough for me.

"I love you," is her only response. She leans forward, kissing me on my lips. "I'm sorry that I ruined our night."

I pull her closer to me. She takes advantage, snuggling into my side. My fingers tingle against the soft skin of her arm.

"Are you kidding? You didn't ruin anything. We have the rest of our lives together. It's not every day that you'll get to witness a child being born up close. A miracle happened here tonight."

She cranes her neck to look up at me. "You know, you say the sweetest things. I want to keep you forever," she jokes as if I'm a stuffed animal that she can toss at any moment.

"Then, forever, you shall have me." It won't be that easy to get rid of me. I brush my lips against her forehead. As long as I have breath, I'm hers.

A thought occurs to me while we're sitting in silence. "Did you really nickname the baby Cloak?"

Sam bursts into laughter, her head straining against my shoulder. It's contagious and causes me to chuckle along with her.

Chapter 20

Samantha

I called Viv Sunday night to let her know that I needed a few days off to help with the babies. Besides that, I simply wasn't ready to leave them yet. Cloak spent three days in the NICU before they released her into the general public. On the fourth day, Lacy and Robert were able to take them home.

It's interesting watching the twins together. The way they cuddle up to each other. Their little coos and cries. I think I'm the one with baby fever.

Brad and I are sitting on the plush carpet with our backs pressed against the long sofa holding the twins. I don't feel bad at all about spoiling them. I keep telling myself that it's

Robert's fault for inviting us to stay. I get the feeling that he and Lacy are grateful for the help. They weren't prepared for the extra blessing. Dad and Margaret also stayed late into the evening yesterday once the babies came home. It's one big family affair.

Lacy and Robert are getting some much-needed sleep after having a rough night and a harrowing couple of days. RJ and Cloak took turns last night, keeping them up. So, I volunteered Brad and me to babysit while they rest. Brad didn't seem to mind and jumped at the chance.

I look down at Cloak relaxing peacefully in my left arm. She's so tiny, but her presence here packs a huge punch. It's too early to know who she'll resemble the most, but those eyes are definitely a product of her mother. Her miniature fingers wrap tightly around my pointer finger. I rub my thumb lightly against her hand. I grin silently when she pouts her little mouth, wondering if her reaction was caused by me or if she's dreaming.

I turn my head to look at Brad and RJ. "How are you doing over there?" I ask him.

"He's my best bud already. Can't you tell?" He chuckles softly.

He looks like a natural holding RJ. Unbothered. Content. Sexy. I take a mental picture of the two of them.

"You're great with them," Brad continues, his eyes scorching my skin.

I'm unbelievably turned on by him right now. I swallow hard to keep the drool from seeping from the corner of my mouth.

"I'd like to thinks so, but this is the easy part," I respond. "Holding, staring, feeding, bathing, playing. All easy. Now raising them, that's the doozy."

"You won't have to do it alone," Brad says, making me question if ovaries can do cartwheels because I'm having a strange reaction to his words.

I have to look away from him. "Leaving them is going to be hard. I didn't expect to be so attached this quickly."

Brad and I are going home tomorrow, and in a couple of weeks, we'll be moving even further away. I'll barely get to see them.

"We'll come to visit as often as possible."

I turn my gaze toward the door when the doorbell sounds. "Must be dad and Margaret," I say.

I stand to go and answer the door, careful not to alarm the baby. I check the peephole to be sure it's them, then open the door.

Dad and Margaret volunteered to pick up all of the little extras that Lacy needed for the babies. Apparently, they came straight over after they were done. They drop everything in the middle of the living room floor, quickly washed their hands, and stole the babies from us. The thieves.

I wasn't sure how to take Margaret in the beginning. I didn't know much about her, but we've become a little more acquainted since then. She's important to dad. They are good together, and she fits right into the family as if she was meant to be here.

With the babies confiscated by their grandparents, Brad and I adopt the task of putting everything away and finishing the setup in the nursery. There's now two of everything significant, lots of onesies and socks, and bottles galore, just to name a few things.

Hours later, Lacy raps on the door jamb to the nursery while Brad and I admire our masterpiece.

"Looks great guys," she says sleepily.

I want to tell her to go back to sleep because her being awake means that I'll have even less time with my niece and nephew once they sense her around.

She walks inside and plops down in one of the rockers. "I didn't mean to sleep that long," Lacy huffs out. "It's taking longer than I thought to rebuild my stamina."

Brad looks between us awkwardly. He leans over and kisses the side of my head. "I'll leave you two alone," he says in a rush to leave the room.

"He's so adorable," Lacy says with a tired laugh.

"He is." I look away from the empty doorway that Brad just went through. I sit next to Lacy in the other rocker. "I think I'm done waiting for the other shoe to drop Lacy. He's given me all the strength that I need to move forward."

"Well, good because I've got my hands full now. I don't have the time to get to know someone new," Lacy cracks.

"No worries there. If by some chance, things don't work out between us, I'll live out the rest of my days as a nun."

Lacy topples over, clutching her belly through the pain caused by her laughter.

"How are you feeling?" I asked her, changing the subject.

"Like I survived being hit by a bus." She smiles. "But those babies out there are totally worth every bit of the pain and sleepless nights. My heart is so full right now. I wish mom were alive to see them." She sighs.

"But you have me instead."

"Grace…" She gives me a look filled with pity.

"It's okay. I'm finally content with being the survivor." I blow out a deep breath and stand, ready to get back to the babies. "I have less than one day to spoil those babies rotten." I reach for her hand, and she stands next to me. "I don't want to waste a minute of it sobbing about what could have been." I chuck my head toward the living room. "Let's get back out there."

Lacy is all too happy to oblige, tired eyes and all.

Midday seemed to come faster than a bullet. Brad and I kept the babies last night to give Lacy and Robert a break. I hardly slept, waking up every other hour to check on them. I doubt that Brad got much rest either. His eyes seem to be watching all three of us every time I opened mine. RJ was the perfect baby, only stirring twice during the night, while

Cloak learned that her lungs are a powerful tool when she wants someone to pick her up, which was pretty much most of the night.

Lacy, Dad, and I fixed a huge breakfast this morning. The three of us together reminded me of past times when we'd have our Friday family nights.

My heart weeps when it's time for us to leave. I'm marveled at how every difficult situation is the hardest thing that I've ever had to go through. One would think that things would get easier with time, and I imagine that's the truth unless it's a new experience. With each new experience comes new feelings at different levels. I think what's the hardest is not knowing how to deal with the emotions caused by the new experience.

That's what I'm feeling now as Brad drives away from my new loves that I've barely gotten a chance to know.

Chapter 21

Bradley

It's been an eventful week, but it feels good to be back home. I can finally concentrate on us again and do what I set out to do. I had planned an elaborate proposal at one of the most sought-after restaurants in the city when Sam received the call from her dad. Plans never seem to work out for me. So, this time, I'm not going to plan it. I'll wait for the right moment and just do it, whether it's tonight, tomorrow, the next day, or the next. She already has my heart. Marriage is just a technicality.

Sam has tried her best to be her usual self since we got back two hours ago, but I can tell that her thoughts are still back in Hinton with those babies. We have a few busy years ahead of us, but I can't wait to have a family of our own. It's strange how the smell of a baby can kick start those parental feelings within you. How a baby can make you love them at first sight.

I wanted to do something to cheer Sam up. So, I ordered one of her favorite foods and had it delivered while she was in the shower. I set the table and light a single candle in the center. I turn the lights down low and wait for her by our bedroom door.

She gasps in surprise when she finally steps out, clad in a light pink thigh-length robe. Her hair is knotted atop her head.

"What are you doing?" She asks.

I wrap my arms around her from behind, kissing her beneath her earlobe. I guide us toward the kitchen slowly. I'm at war with the direction we're headed when all I want to do is turn around and take her to bed.

"Trying to cheer you up," I answer. "You haven't been yourself since we got back."

"Is it that noticeable?" She doesn't try to deny my accusation.

I unleash my hold to step in front of her. I grab her hand and continue toward the kitchen. "I have just the thing to bring you back to me."

"Is that so?"

I smirk.

She stops when we reach our destination. She peers inside like she's afraid to enter.

"When did you...?" Words seem to fail her while staring at the romantic setup.

"Are you hungry?" I ask.

She nods and steps inside. When we sit down at the bar, she begins to giggle while staring at my makeshift food covers. I had taken the plastic covers used in the microwave to hide our dinner like they do in the fancy restaurants.

"You certainly haven't lost your flair for the dramatic," she said, amused.

"Not much gets lost when it comes to you."

I wait for her reaction as she lifts the lid from her dish.

"My favorite. And you even remembered the ketchup."

"I'll never forget the ketchup." We both laugh and begin eating.

When dinner is over, I suggest that we watch a movie. Sam is surprised at my choice and even teases me about it. I have to remind her that I grew up with Gin, and even though I didn't like most of the movies that she watched, there were a few that stuck with me.

"Fools Rush In? Seriously?" Sam grins at me with mock criticism.

I shrug. "I happen to like it."

"You have me curious, Mr. Pierce, but I'll hold all questions until after the movie." She pulls me down on the couch next to her.

I lean back and wrap my arms around her, taking in the smell of her ivory scented body wash. I nuzzle into her neck, eliciting a tiny giggle from her. My cock twitches in my sweatpants, eagerly trying to reach her to no end. I'm beginning to rethink the whole movie thing and skip straight to the end.

"Brad," she says coyly. "The movie's starting."

I nibble on her earlobe, giving her something to think about. "Before this night is over," I promise, whispering softly in her ear.

Sam bites on her bottom lip. Her face turns a shade darker, but she doesn't chance a look at me. She knows me well, and she knows that looking at me while I'm standing at attention will only escalate things quickly. I glance down at myself, giving him the same promise, assuring him that she is worth the wait.

Even though Sam gave me a hard time about the movie, I can tell that she's into it too. The way she rests her head on my shoulder and snuggles into my side. The way her legs comfortably lap over mine. The soft caress of her hand on my bare chest. Yeah, she's into the movie and driving me insane in the process.

Sam wipes at her eyes when the credits start to roll. She peers up at me with sad eyes. "For a guy, you sure know how to pick a good movie," she sniffles.

I press my lips to her temple. "Believe it or not, there's a reason that I picked that particular movie."

Her brows rise slightly. Her curiosity piqued. "I can't wait to hear the story behind this one." She untangles her legs from mine and sits up, twisting her body to face me.

"There is no story. For me, it's more about what the movie represents. It kind of reminds me of us."

She tilts her head to the side in interest. "Are you calling us a couple of fools?" she asks jokingly.

I almost say yes, because, in hindsight, that's what we are. A couple of fools who fell in love. Before I speak, I consider my explanation.

"Isn't everyone a fool for something? I won't deny that I am. I've been a fool for you from the moment your voice pierced my ears. We rushed into this relationship slowly and carefully. Neither one of us knowing what the other was made of."

I pause and get down on one knee. Sam's eyes widen, her hand rising to cover her mouth. I slip my hand underneath the sofa to retrieve the small box.

"The thing is Sam; it doesn't matter that I don't know everything about you. What does matter is the fact that I want to spend the rest of my life learning. I want you to teach me, baby."

I flip the lid open on the box, revealing the gold band inside. A tear slips down Sam's face.

"Samantha Grace Young, will you marry me?"

Her tears are falling freely now. She touches her forehead to mine. The breath rushes out of her in waves.

After a few moments, she lifts her head to look at me, and her breathing calms to a steady pace.

"Yes," she croaks out.

Her salty lips press firmly against mine.

"Yes," she says again. "I want you to teach me."

I pull the ring out of the box and slide it onto her finger. I join her on the sofa and pull her over to straddle me. I kiss her with ease, slipping my hand beneath the tail of her robe. Her thighs are warm to my touch.

"I think it's time to make good on my promise," I say, lifting my hips to meet her sheer covered center.

"I think you're right," she says breathily. She grinds against me teasingly, causing me to swell beneath her.

Before this night is over, she'll be wrapped tightly around me. I'll be deep inside of her. Class is in session. I'll teach her. She'll teach me. The rest of our lives will be a learning experience, starting with my new favorite subject. Sex Education. The adult version.

Chapter 22

Samantha

I keep staring at the ring on my finger and thinking about last night. Brad's proposal was perfect and not at all what I was expecting. I pull the ring from my finger to read the inscription for the umpteenth time today.

It reads in bold print, *MY YELLOW*.

I sigh heavily, happily. I haven't been able to concentrate at all today at work. The reality of my life is beginning to sink in. I just got engaged. Brad and I are moving. I have to apply to another school. I have to find another job. And lastly, I have to break the news to Viv and Jeff.

It's a thought that saddens me. They have been so good to me, giving me the chance of a lifetime. I've been able to study under one of the best, and we've become good friends. It will be hard finding that again and starting all over, but I have to try.

My gut feeling tells me that Brad is the one I'm supposed to spend my life with. I didn't have definitive plans to remain here when school was over. This place was always a stepping stone for me. Only now, I know why.

"Is there something you want to get off of your chest, honey?" Viv sidles up next to me. "You're smiling one minute and frowning the next. It's frustrating to watch." She slaps my arm playfully with the kitchen towel.

"There is actually. I need to talk to you and Jeff after work."

She looks at me, skeptically. "This wouldn't have anything to do with your dinner date last week, would it? You two rushed out of here in a hurry. By the way, how are those babies?" Viv fires off question after question, not letting me get a word in.

I stare at her until she finishes.

"The babies are great. I miss them already," I answer. "It's crazy how easily everything is changing. How quickly things are happening." I rest my hand on the countertop.

"Is that an engagement ring?" Viv blurts out suddenly. She snatches my hand, pulling it close to her face. "Good looking and has taste. This is beautiful, honey." She pats my hand steps back on her side of the steel table and continues to peel her potatoes.

"Thank you."

I make myself busy preparing for opening in less than an hour. Viv doesn't ask me any more questions, and I try not to flip flop my emotions to keep her from asking.

We have a full house, just like every other night. And as usual, lots of excited hopefuls. When the last couple leaves, and we close the doors for the night, my heartbeat picks up nervously with me thinking about what I must do.

The vibe is solemn when I walk into Jeff's office. I don't know if they suspect what's coming or not. I sit down beside Viv across from Jeff.

"How was the proposal?" Jeff asks.

"It went great," I say, raising my hand to show him my new jewel.

Something flashes in his eyes before he crooks a smile. "Just as I suspected it would." He leans back in his chair and crosses his arms over his chest. "So, what's this all about?"

"As you know, I'm getting married," I say, lifting my hand again for emphasis.

"Are you pregnant, honey?" Viv cuts in.

I chuckle at her bluntness. It's one of the things that I'll miss the most about her.

"No, nothing like that. Brad has been offered the job of a lifetime. So, we'll be moving to Munik soon. Which means that I'll have to put in my notice here."

Viv is rendered speechless for the first time since I met her.

Jeff nods. "I'm sorry to see you go," he says. "I guess congratulations are in order. Any idea when the move is going to happen?"

"In a few weeks, I assume. We haven't ironed out all of the details yet. I just wanted you to be aware in case you needed to replace me."

"No one will ever replace you. You were a favor for a friend." Viv winks. "I may need someone to help prep in the mornings," she directs at Jeff. "But only part-time."

Jeff nods and directs his attention back to me. "If you need help finding a job, I may know someone in Munik that can help."

"Thank you. That would be great," I respond.

"I'll make a phone call to my contact tomorrow. Let us know as soon as possible when you'll be leaving. In the meantime, Viv, I'll place an ad for a temp to help out."

I don't know what I was expecting when I walked in. I guess I had anticipated some backlash and some angry looks, but they surprised me. I truly am going to miss it here.

When I leave work, I call Em to tell her the news. I feel guilty that she wasn't one of the first that I told about my engagement, but she doesn't have to know that. I haven't even told dad and Lacy yet. I'll make that call first thing in the morning.

"Hello." She answers chipper as if it's not almost midnight.

"Hey Em, do you have a few minutes to talk?"

"Sure. What's up?" I hear rumbling in the background, and I hope that I didn't interrupt anything important. The sound of a door closing reaches me through the phone.

"I probably should have done this in person, but I couldn't hold it in any longer."

"Ooh, do tell," she says.

"Brad and I are engaged."

She sucks in a sharp breath. I can sense her excitement through the phone.

"Oh my gosh!" She shouts in a hushed tone. "You're getting married." She pauses. "Wait, you're not pregnant, are you?"

I laugh. *Why does everyone ask that question,* I think to myself. "No, I'm not pregnant."

"Well, in that case, I accept."

"Accept what?" I ask, confused.

"I am your maid of honor, right?"

I shake my head at her assumption. "Of course, you are. I can't think of anyone better to hold that title."

"Eek!" She screeches in my ear.

"There's one more thing, Em. We're moving in a few weeks."

She's quiet for a moment. "But why?" She questions.

"Brad accepted a new job that requires him to move," I say.

"And you can't stand the thought of him leaving you behind." She finishes my thought. "I don't blame you. I've always said that he's a good guy. If you can't see a future without him, and he makes you happy, even when you're mad at him, then go for it. I'll miss you around here, though."

"You'll still see me. We have a family here. And you'll hear from me even more."

We talk more about my engagement, and I agree to call her soon to go over wedding plans before we end the call.

When I enter our apartment, Brad is waiting for me. He must sense that my mind is tired, and I have no conversation left in me. Not tonight. He carries me to our bedroom, where I change into something comfortable. Then I climb into bed beside him. He comforts me and reminds me of his love. Soon after, I drift off to sleep.

Chapter 23

Bradley

Sam has been tied up most of the week trying to get things in order for our move. Jeff, her boss, was kind enough to help snag her an interview once we move. She found a suitable school in Munik that offers the courses she needs to graduate next year. Everything seems to be falling into place.

I know she said that it's her choice to come with me, but the guilt still pricks my skin every now and again. I wish there was something that I could do to make the transition easier for her. I'm hoping that my surprise will make up for everything she's going through to be with me. It will be a few months before I can give it to her, but my fingers are crossed that she'll love it.

I've found an apartment in a nice neighborhood in Munik. It's not as elaborate as the one David offered, but it's worthy enough for my Sam. And it's only temporary until we move into something better.

Sam told her dad and Lacy about our plans on Monday. He called me right after to offer his congratulations and a warning, to which he has nothing to worry about. I would never intentionally hurt Sam. If I had any doubt, I would never have asked her to marry me.

Today, Val is coming over to let us know what happened with Garrett. We probably could have discussed it over the phone, but she insisted on seeing her best friend one last time before she leaves tomorrow. To be honest, Sam said that she truly didn't care anymore. Her main focus is us, our wedding, and our future. Everything that he did, she let it all go. She forgave him so that we could move forward.

I ask myself daily. How did I get so lucky? How could a boy who despised love grow up to be a man overflowing with it?

"Brad, Valerie's here," Sam calls through the apartment.

The two of them are chatting at the bar in the kitchen. Sam's eyes light up when she sees me, drawing Val's attention to me.

"Bradley. I was just congratulating Samantha on your engagement. You've surprised me yet again, my friend," she says. "It's about time that you came to your senses before someone else snagged her."

I step next to Sam, placing my hand on her back. "I would never let that happen," I respond. I stare at Sam. Her eyes sparkle, throwing off that vibe that I love. I don't even think she realizes it's happening. I clear my throat and look away.

"That's what love looks like," Val says.

"Why don't you tell us about Garrett," I say to Val.

"There's not much to tell. I believe Garrett has fallen for me. We've gotten very close, closer than I wanted to be. Then I did as we planned. I told him that we'd finally closed on the house. That I was leaving. He asked me to stay. He never said that he loved me, but I felt it. There's no hiding something like that. Of course, I told him that I couldn't stay. That I had to get back to my life. That this thing between us was never meant to last. I think it's safe to say that he's crushed. I haven't heard from him since, but I saw him with some other chick just last night."

Sam doesn't seem happy with the news. If anything, there's a hint of regret in her gaze. I, on the other hand, think that he got less than he deserved. A broken heart doesn't seem to be enough for the crime that he committed.

"I really wanted to come over and say goodbye," Val continues. "Leave on a good note. This will probably be the last time that we talk for a while. You're practically a married man now." She bumps my shoulder. "And no wife wants her husband conversing with the ex; best friend or not."

"You'll have to leave an address," Sam says. "For the wedding invite. I wouldn't dare keep his best friend away. That's if you want to come."

"I would love to. I need to see this with my own eyes to believe it," Valerie jokes.

"I'm sure I'll be speaking those same words to you one day. I know it's going to happen for you, even if you don't believe it."

"This," Val says, motioning to Sam and me, "will never be me. Ever," she stresses.

A smile creeps onto Sam's lips, and I know just what she's thinking. We both believed something similar at one point in time. Now look at us, hopelessly in love, unbreakable, and nothing can tear us apart.

Chapter 24

6 Months Later
Samantha

After the move, the planning, the stressing, we are finally here. Our wedding day.

Though I miss my friends at Reynaldo's, I love my new job. Some employees weren't so welcoming in the beginning, but we've all come to an understanding of sorts now.

School has been a breeze. It's much less stressful not having to worry about running into Garrett at every turn. The only thing I miss about my old school is being able to see Em, but we talk at least three times per week.

Brad kept his word. Once a month, we go and visit the twins, and each time I don't want to leave. Each time they've gained more pounds or picked up a new trait. RJ, surprisingly, is the quiet one. And Cloak, contrary to her nickname, refuses to be in the shadows. She demands to be seen and heard.

Em was crucial in helping with plans for our wedding. We even had help from Gin. Lacy wasn't able to help much with the twins requiring so much time, but her advice and input were more than enough.

I touch my mother's crowned comb on my head. "Something old. Check."

I run my fingers along Lacy's white laced veil. "Something Borrowed. Check."

I check my bra to make sure that the small pin is still attached. "Something blue. Check."

Lastly, I stare at my dress in the mirror. "Something new. Check."

My dress is simply beautiful. I chose a sheath look. It's white with shimmering yellow bands, one in the back and one in the front, holding the thick straps together. A small portion of my belly peeks out in the front. The hem is only a millimeter away from the ground. The attached chapel train is coated in yellow to match the bands but without all of the glitz.

"Are you ready, Grace?" Lacy comes to stand next to me. I chose her to be my Matron of Honor. Nathan happily took on the role of best man, and Phillip is one of the groomsmen.

"I couldn't be more ready," I respond.

"Sammy. You look beautiful."

I turn to face the door when I hear my dad's voice behind me.

Em fluffs out my train and gives me an air kiss. "Showtime," she says. "See you out there."

"I guess this is it," Lacy says, following Em's lead. She tucks a bouquet of sunflowers into my hands and gives me a barely-there kiss on my cheek before leaving dad and me alone.

"How's my Sammy today," dad says once the room is clear.

My smile brightens. "Sammy's doing just fine, dad."

"Your mother would have been so proud," he says. "I'm proud. I think you have yourself a good man in Bradley." He pauses. "But if by any chance that should change, you know where to find me."

"Thanks, dad. For everything." I respond like this is the end of our father-daughter relationship.

Dad walks me down the aisle and gives Brad my hand when instructed. From the moment our hands touch, I block out everything and everyone else in attendance. It's just Brad and me. We say the traditional vows that I barely remember saying. What I do remember is Brad's unwavering smile, the way he held my hand, and slid the ring onto my finger, the candor of his words when he said, *"I do,"* and the tender kiss that he placed on my lips to solidify our union.

The reception followed promptly after we took pictures with the wedding party. Our first dance is unlike any other dance we've had before. I've always felt protected in Brad's arms, but this is different. He's the same Brad, but with extra everything. Extra protection. More intensity. Overpowering love. There's a fierceness in his stare that dares anyone to harm me. It seems as if the moment my dad gave him my hand, it all happened in an instant.

"Are you going to tell me where we're going?" I ask out of habit as we sway back and forth on the dance floor.

I don't know why I bother. Brad is never going to tell me. He is the king of surprises.

His fingers graze the bare skin on my back. "If I tell you, I'll have to kill you." He chuckles.

"So soon after our, I do's?" I question.

"I think I'll keep the secret. I like having you around," Brad whispers. "There is one thing that I can tell you," he continues as his hand creeps lower on my back.

I let him have his way in front of all of our friends and family, knowing it would be useless to try and stop him. If anything, it would worsen his reaction. He's made it clear to me on several occasions that he doesn't care who's watching. So, as long as he doesn't try to strip me bare in public, I approve.

"What's that?" I ask.

His hand stops just below my waistline. His lips linger below my earlobe for a moment. "You won't be disappointed."

A small bead of liquid trickles out of me, staining my panties. "Brad," I say against his chest.

"What is it, baby?"

I sense the smug grin on his face without seeing it. His impish tone says it all.

"I think it's time that we get out of here."

"If that's what you want," he says, knowing that he's lured me in.

I can't wait to have him all to myself.

Chapter 25

Bradley

For our honeymoon, I surprised Sam with a trip to Catalina Island. Needless to say, we didn't do much sightseeing on our four-day trip. Most of our time was spent soaking up the sun at the beach and lounging around in bed.

Sam crashed as soon as we got back. She was too nervous to sleep on the plane. I guess all the built-up anxiety drained her.

While she was sleeping, I took a drive to check on her surprise. They assured me that it would be ready when we returned. Satisfied by what I see, I return home to get Sam.

She's still asleep, and it takes her nearly an hour to wake up.

"Good. You're finally awake." I tell her when her eyes crack open.

I may have hurried along the process by sitting next to her on the bed.

"I'm so tired," she yawns.

"I know, but I have something to show you. Your wedding gift."

She slowly climbs to a sitting position on the bed. "Okay. Where is it?"

"You'll have to leave the house for this one. We're going for a ride."

"But we just got back," she whines.

"It's not far. I promise. Then you can sleep as much as you want afterward."

Sam begrudgingly puts her shoes on and follows me to the car. Twelve minutes later, we pull up to my Grandparent's old house by the lake. It's the same house where I brought Sam months ago. It's the house that my grandparents gave to me when they moved away. For years it's been sitting, waiting for me to decide what to do with it.

When I first acquired it, I had no idea why they chose me, the boy who didn't believe in love. The boy who never thought of having a family. I didn't understand until now. Somehow, they knew that my views would change. They knew that I would meet the woman of my dreams. They knew that one day I would want a family of my own. They knew that this day would come, long before I dared to dream.

Her eyes widen when I park and take the key out of the ignition. I get out and open her door for her to come with me. We walk hand in hand to the front porch where I stop. Sam still hasn't said one word. Her free hand rests over her heart.

"Do you like it?" I ask her, critiquing every emotion she portrays.

"What is this, Brad? What have you done?" She asks as she looks around at the newly renovated house.

I instructed the crew to fix everything up, but keep the colors neutral. When Sam is ready, she can pick her own colors, her own drapes, her own furniture. The only room that I've furnished is our bedroom.

"This was my grandparent's house. They gave it to me. Now it's ours."

"Brad. I don't know what to say. When did you have time to do all of this?"

"Come with me," I say.

I take her inside and show her around. Then we continue on to the back of the house. I spread out a blanket on the ground for us to sit on near the lake.

"For the longest time, I didn't know what to do with this place. It was only a memory box," I tell Sam, taking her hand in mine. "The two weeks that I spent away from you were the hardest, longest two weeks of my life. It made me realize what I wanted to do with this house. I knew then that I wanted to create new memories here, with you. So, I started working on it immediately."

"What I said to you when we were here before, I meant every word," I continue. "Things have changed. We've changed. We can never go back to the way it used to be. What I imagined in the beginning for this place will never be." I pause. "But we can move forward and make it better than I ever imagined."

Sam climbs onto my lap, straddling me. Her eyes glisten in the sunlight. Her hands cradle my cheeks as her lips slowly descend upon mine.

"Thank you. I love it," she says when we pull apart. "I love it. I love you. You're under my skin Bradley Pierce," she whispers.

"And I don't mind living there with you, Mrs. Pierce," I finish. "You will always be My Yellow."

The End.

Acknowledgments

For me, it all starts with an idea. The idea leads to an image. I loved writing this series, and I loved every single cover. So, thank you, Tracie Douglas, at Dark Water Covers for taking those images and bringing them to life.

To Nicole Townsend Browne, my second set of hands, thank you for jumping on board with this series and helping out in other areas. It's a pleasure to be working with you.

To Karen Barr, Thank you for being my second set of eyes and a listening ear.

To Parker's Angels, advance readers, and all individuals & blogs involved, thank you for continuing on this journey with me.

Author's Note

Everything that anyone does, big or small, plays a huge part in an author's success. I appreciate you all so very much. Thanks for coming along with me on my journey. If you enjoyed reading my book, please consider posting a review on your preferred site; and don't forget to tell your friends about me.

Until Next Time...

About the Author

Angela K. Parker is a country girl with a big heart. She's a South Carolina native with a passion for writing, reading, music, & math. When she's not engaged in any of the above, she's spending time with her family or catching up on the latest movies. She's always had a very active imagination. Now she's putting it to good use.

Connect with the Author

Website: www.angelakparker.com

Email: angelaparkerauthor@gmail.com

Made in the USA
Middletown, DE
30 September 2023